CISCO RIDES SLICK

S. SOUTHCOTT

This is a work of fiction. All characters and events portrayed in this book are either products of the author's imagination or are used fictitiously.

Cisco Rides Slick

A Star Brand Dime Novel
Star Brand Publications

ISBN 978-0-578-02172-0

Printed in the United States of America

Acknowledgments

I thank the Good Lord for giving me a rock to stand on when I was tired of jumping in the mud.

I want to thank my two imaginative and slightly eccentric children Crystil and Jakub for helping me with the characters of Veloria and Vincent Beauregarde.

Thanks to my friend Judy aka "Texas Annie" for giving me the inspiration for the character of Texas.

Thank you Charles, Mom, Al, Aunt Diane, and my NewHeart family for all of your support.

I would like to especially thank everyone who read the first book, *On the Trail with Cisco Peach*. You're much needed input and support helped me to be a better writer. Keep it comin'!

Introduction

It all started with a sepia tone picture of a young girl in men's clothing. She was armed with a rifle and pistol. The scowl she wore didn't quite fit with her sweet oval face and perfect lips. She was serving time in Yuma prison for holding up a stage. She gave herself the title of "Bandit Queen". Her name was Pearl Hart.

I couldn't get this picture out of my mind and because I believe that all answers to life's questions can be answered at the local library, did some research. My first book, *On the Trail with Cisco Peach*, was built upon the character of Pearl. More research led me to discover many other ladies of the west who had stories of their own. I was delighted in particular with the rough and tumble women of the Wild West shows and early rodeo whose stories have helped me to write this book. These ladies blazed a fearless trail into the male dominated arena of bronc and bull riding. They did so at the cost of public opinion (this was the Victorian era after all), health, and sometimes even their lives. A group of the early rodeo gals dubbed themselves the "Wild Bunch" and there was no doubt that it was true.

I hoped to honor their contribution to women's history which is weaved into the fabric of the history of America itself, whether we hear about it or not.

Lastly, I would like to note that I took some liberty for the sake of the story with the appearance of Annie

Oakley in Omaha. Her first appearance with the Wild West was actually in Louisville Kentucky 1885.

This one is for the "Wild Bunch". If I was around during their time, I would have been right up there with them.

"What we want to do is give our women even more liberty than they have. Let them do any kind of work they see fit, and if they do it as well as men, give them the same pay."

-Buffalo Bill Cody 1899

"It didn't take guts for me to ride bulls; it took guts for me to buck the people who didn't want me to do it."

-Jonnie Jonckowski
Two-Time World Champion Bull Rider

1

She could hear the creak of straining leather in her glove as it gripped the rope. The pounding of her heart was all around her ears and bottled beneath her ten gallon hat. She could feel their eyes on her. A whistle floated in the air. There was a loud boom as one of the bronc's hoofs slammed into the side of the arena.

"That's right pard, you git good and mad like me." She spoke in a low tone through clenched teeth and waved her free hand above her head.

There was a brief pause when the animal was set free. It hung in the air and floated there suspended. She lifted her chin and met the smirks and smiles with a touch to her hat brim and held on. The crowd went wild.

*

It all started with a cloud of dust coming on up over the hill. A couple of the girls and myself were leaning on the fence and lookin' over our herd of mares and spring foals after a hard days work. We've been in the horse business for a couple of years now and done mighty well for ourselves. You take into consideration that we yanked the place into shape from a former sport house, now that my friend was work! Still, ranchin' seemed to fit us like a glove. Those that stayed on with us gave with whole heart and both hands. I guess when you've had it bad like most of us did a shot at something good sounds even better. No one had come to dance the hemp jig with us so far. We heard tales of a hangin' that went down with a lady rancher and her husband but we had Leon (who we called Chop) around. Book and I always wore the hats so maybe they figured not to fool with those that had the protection of a few extra hands, not to mention guns.

The dust was still coming. Colonel Redbird came up on us from behind with her usual flare for grand entrance and uncanny ability to read dust clouds. She announced, "Here comes Della gals. Let's up and have us some good dinner and conversation. I'll have Chop fix up somethin' extra special!"

Maybe I otta explain the Colonel before I go on. She is a former madam and a mountain of a woman for sure. She wears her flamin' red hair in a pile on her head with no neck between her jaw and shoulders to speak of. She usually sports a big cigar between her teeth and wears men's trousers tucked into her tall cavalry boots. Her bull dog business sense keeps the Flying Bird Ranch up and running like a fine-tuned timepiece. Her booming voice is usually followed by her big heart and generally good nature...unless you cross her. Trust me, you don't take a stroll on the bad side of an ornery horse and you don't make an enemy of the Colonel. I am glad to say that she has been a good friend to me and my friend Book these few years.

I otta explain my good friend Book while I'm at it. Talking Book and I crossed paths when I was on the run from a bad situation. My Ma helped me escape from my drunken, family beatin' Pa. I took to the trail wearing men's clothes she left for me along with a set of Colt Thunderer pistols. Down the road a spell, I came upon a run down shack and found two men mistreating an Indian girl they were keeping inside. Let's just say they will never hurt anyone again. The story goes that she was the daughter of a chief called Medicine Hair. Her tribe had traded her for a load of guns because she had spent some time living with missionaries. The fact is that they had no use for the things she learned from the Good Book. The girl was soon to be my good friend and riding partner. Our adventures on the trail led us here to the Flying Bird Ranch where we work as hands. That's the short version of course which leads us now to the dust cloud fast approaching.

The face that started to appear from the swirl was smiling, waving, and shouting something that we couldn't quite hear yet. We soon knew who it was for sure. When it came closer, it was easier to make out.

"Wooo Ha! Let er buck gals! Old D's back at the ranch!" There was a fringed glove waving a tall hat.

I can tell you with a heavy heart that from the look of D's get up, "civilized" society had found a way to make a skirt into pants for riding. The puzzled looks around the group were proof enough that the rest had the same notion. I guess we got used to wearing pants and never gave thought to it. Who in their right mind would try and do the work we did in skirts!? Hers were sort of

3

big-legged jobs made from leather with long fringe around the bottom that made sort of a swish sound. They had a row of silver buttons running down both sides of the front. She even had on a vest to match the pants, right down to the swish fringe. Book was much impressed with the beadwork in her hat band and matching arm bands to keep her shirt sleeves in check. Her kerchief was red with fancy stitching and looked like it cost a few more coins than calico. Our eyes got wide as plates when we spied her spurs. Big sliver spurs with jingle bobs and hand made leather straps with stars carved into the sides. She just sat there with her big-toothed grin atop her pretty rust colored gelding and sparkled in the setting sun.

We stood there gaping while the Colonel took a quick up and down inventory. She took a puff of her smoke, blowing it up and into the breeze. She winked at D and said, "Well, I can hardly keep from shadin' my eyes from all the show sparkle you got goin' on these days! Come on down and let's have a look at ya."

D swung down from her horse and held her arms out. Her golden hair was braided and hung to the sides. The fringe from her outfit swung as she twirled around in a circle. "Well now Colonel. What do ya say? Ain't I somethin'?"

The Colonel shook her head and said, "You're somethin' alright. Now come on in and sit down with me and tell me all about it."

Chop came busting out of the ranch door just then, wiping his hands in a kitchen rag and smiling his big smile. D ran over and gave him a big hug. "I sure do miss your cookin' when I'm out, you big bear. Let's eat!"

Our Flying Bird Ranch outfit wasn't as big as some outfits that raised cattle. We started out with the Colonel and a couple of her girls who wanted to stay on with us after we helped close down the Bird House, a different kind of business I'm glad I never got caught up in. We were all washed up and crammed around the long kitchen table leaning in toward D. I don't know if I was more excited about the smells coming from the cook top or about the tales we had in store for us.

D scooted into her spot with the cling of jingle bob spurs under her chair. This move helped to emphasize the fact that she had us at full attention. She had taken off her gloves and rolled back her sleeves and I could see the scars and fading bruises on her hands and arms. She wasn't a fair beauty but still the same, her round and moon-like face lit up when she smiled. Her turned up nose had a faint splash of faded freckles. When she spoke, her blue-green eyes were full of devilment.

"I can tell you gals that I have had my fun with the rank ponies that those boys tried to throw my way. Why, you would think they don't want us to outride 'em at all. All the bangin' round does take a toll on the body though. You'd think I'd gone and done enough to myself by now without takin' on the broncs." She turned to the Colonel and gave a wink. "My, but you should hear the crowds yell for us!"

This last statement raised up a question for me so I cut in, "Crowds? What kind a big ranch you ridin' at?"

She looked at me like I had just thrown down my winning hand and none of the suits matched. She scrunched up her brow and said, "You all don't get out much around here do ya? I'm ridin' for Bill Cody hisself and his Wild West. I just got off the train and rode up over the hill. You mean to tell me that none of ya have heard of Buffalo Bill and his Wild West?"

The Colonel cut in while we commenced at looking bewildered. "Well I can say I heard rumors of Cody's outfit. Maybe you can give us a little more to go on here like where have ya been and what have ya been doin', exit-tera."

D reached up and pushed her hat back. Her moon face lit up again and she started in. "A while back I was helpin' out a ranch and takin' in some extra pocket change by breakin' some rough horses. Those old boys' ideas about females and horses were shut as soon as they saw I could ride almost any outlaw they had on hand. One day it was business as usual and this fella comes up to me and tells me he is a scout for Bill Cody! He says he can use a gal like me in his show. I figured I could make more money if I joined up so next thing ya know I was on a train to Omaha!"

Right about then Keyes bumped into the kitchen from upstairs. She was a gal that worked playing piano at the old Bird House. She cut a slim, fine lady frame, with a reddish gold wave of hair that was pulled back. You could hear her Southern upbringing linger in her voice. She was wearin' a long skirt with a pretty flower blouse tucked in. She preferred this way of dressing which was more of a liking to most of the population of females than the trousers we wore. She knew how to put on the pants when it came to rough work though.

"My my now, Della, but don't you look a sight! How you been, gal?" She scooted on over, bent down, kissed her long time friend on the cheek, and squeezed up D's freckles. Her hat popped right off and rolled like tumbleweed across the wood floor.

"I was just lettin' these here gals in on the details of my travels. Why don't ya squeeze yourself up and I'll go on?" She squeezed and we went on.

"Like I was sayin', I got to Nebraska and got off the train and came up over this hill into a big meadow. There was a city of tents and animals! Every which way there was the hustle of activity, people in outfits from all over the world, buffalo, elk, so many horses, why one gal passed by me totin' a little ol' wolf cub!

"I smelled things I never smelled and saw things I could not even begin to tell ya about! You would have to see it for your own self. I was led up to a tent and who do you think stepped right out to say hello to your old friend? Why it was William F. Cody, Buffalo Bill hisself!" There was an intake of breath from around the group and a high whistle from the Colonel.

Along came a round of ricocheting questions from all angles. "Was he tall? What'd he say? How did he talk? What's he look like? Did he have a gun? What'd you do?"

She waited for a quiet in the storm, "Buffalo Bill is tall and a mighty fine talker. He stepped out of his tent, gripped my glove in his with a smile, and said, 'I am delighted to meet you young lady. My man tells me you break a mean bronc. Right now we have another young lady you might have heard of by the name of Annie, who dazzles the rest of us with her sharp shooting. We have been thinking over the possibility of adding some more ladies to our program, which is why you have caught our attention. Do you think you might be interested in demonstrating your riding talent? I am inclined to believe that women have as much place in the Wild West as men and am willing to pay equally for equal work. How does that sound?'

D said, "I tell ya I just stood there starin' at the man. Like I was sayin', he was tall and had on beaded buckskin top to bottom. He had tall black boots that went above his knees. He had wavy long hair and a beard. He had a little of the devil behind his eyes that sparkled a mite. He was all gentlemen I can tell ya. Before you know it I was noddin' my head up and down and tellin' him ok. Equal pay! Next I was led around by one of his men to get a look at what I was signin' up with and given the rules. Bill don't like his people causin' trouble so the outfit is pretty clean. Him and his man Nate call it a *high-toned* program."

I cut in with, "Are there any other gals ridin' like you? I figure it might be a little rough in those skirts you got on."

She got real serious and looked me straight in the eye. "Cisco, that's a funny thing you ask. There's only a couple of us right now but we are tryin' to kick the door open for the others that come behind us. Some people aren't ready yet for girls, who don't ride sidesaddle-like, and sometimes we get a little trouble for it, but you should hear the crowd. They love us mostly. Someday I bet there'll be some of us wearin' pants even! Right now we figure to make a sort of deal and split up our skirts. We can decorate 'em up though with this fringe and whatnot. They sure gave us some fine horses like that there geldin' I rode in on. Maybe you should come and see for yourself. Hey! You gotta see that Annie. She can shoot better then any man I ever saw! We can bring Book too. Hey Book! You should see the Indian camp they got!"

At this news, Book sat straight up in her chair and snapped to attention. She cut in with "What kind of camp do they have?"

Times were changin' on the plains. The buffalo were dwindled down to a trickle and most of the Indian population was being moved onto reservations and "given" land by the government. Of course there were a few stray bands that refused the "offer" and were making trouble here or there. We hadn't seen any members of Book's tribe of late and she was wondering what had happened to them. Her father was a local chief and we had a deal with him to not raid our horses. Nobody so far asked about the ranch having an Indian hand so we just kept on goin' like no one would. I wasn't too sure about traveling outside the ranch but I kept it to myself.

Our talk was cut short by a pile of biscuits that was plopped down on each side of the table. We had stewed meat, cut greens from the garden patch, the said biscuits, and a steaming hot apple treat sitting up on the window sill to cool down. I tell ya, I know not how our friend and cook Chop can make things taste the way they do but not a one of us could make a peep after we started in eating.

We call him Chop but his real name is Lee On and he comes from some little place in China. He came to San Francisco in California to what they call the "Gold Mountain" with a couple of family members. They brought Chinese medicine and hoped to make their fortune like so many others only to find heartache. People wanted opium and alcohol, not real help or health. He saved the Colonel's life when she was almost murdered by some so-called local lawmen.

I have never met a man in my life more educated and loyal than Lee, not to mention his cookin'. We were all lucky to have him around.

I can say that D had planted a small seed of a curious nature in Book. She had a tree growing by the time she talked to me later after dinner.

Now there have only been a few cross conversations between my good friend and riding partner and myself. One was when we signed on with the Flying Bird. I was on the run from my past and a killer who had me in his sights after I shot his brother. I had no call to stay on with the Colonel, who I didn't know, and a bunch of newly ex-working girls to start a horse ranch. Two was right about now when she had a notion to travel by train to Omaha to see D's Wild West. Like I say, the seed grew into a tree and was now a full-fledged forest. Her eyes were blazing with a war party glow when she brought it up.

"I can see no difference whether we travel by train or no. D says many people travel to see.."

I cut her off with my usual speech of the glass half empty variety. "Oh sure! D says this and says that! Am I the only one who is thinkin' about you? Book! I know you want to see what's happening with your people. Have you figured that things ain't so good right now for you all? What if we get out there and the government tries to give you an invite to one of those reservations of theirs? What if they take you away from me...*us*?"

Right about now my face was burnin' hot, my throat was tightening up, and water was threatening to spill over the dam. She looked me over and with her usual tone of hope glimmering, she said, "We will have to trust in the Father and His care for me...*us*"

*

A lone woman drug her shoes through the heat and dust toward the valley. Her bag felt like it had been loaded down with rocks. If she could just get over this last hill she could make it. One more step. Salty beads of perspiration stung her eyes and blurred her vision. One more step. How could anyone feel any better than an animal after riding that train? Shoved into the back with the heat and the dust working its way through your clothes and skin. Why the smell was enough to knock a dog off a gut wagon! She swiped at her forehead only making a muddy streak. One more step. When was the last time she slept? Then, there it was, spreading out below the hill. The Flying Bird Ranch.

"Well shore nuff." Her shoe caught on a stone and sent her tumbling down the hill.

*

I can tell you right about now I was not happy about this plan. We were packing up our bags to take on our "trip" to see the Wild West in Omaha. I had a sour face on in a crowd of giddy well wishers.

D was cluing me in on the particulars of train travel. "Now Cisco, ya'all are gonna need dusters for the trip. Just trust me on this one. Don't flash any finery and keep your money close. You ever heard of a cardsharp? We'll have to keep an eye on you." She pointed at me.

I answered in my best smart alec tone, "What in Pike's name would I do with any finery! Colonel, do you hear this..this dust bein' thrown around here?! Any more wind and we could have a tornado!"

I looked over at Book and I could tell she thought this was all very amusing. D looked at Book for back up.

"Book, is it gonna be this way the whole trip? All I'm doin' here is givin' a few pointers." She frowned in my direction with her freckles scrunched up above her turned up nose.

I piped up with my finger pointed in her direction, "I'll give you a pointer. You can take your…"

Our conversation was cut off by a loud thump and a general commotion going on down stairs. We all rushed out to the top of the stairs to see what went on.

4

Her dust-caked eyes cracked open like a deep desert canyon. The faces stood around her in a circle with wide eyes. She could only think of one thing to say, "Thank the Good Lord I made it." She fell back into unconsciousness.

Those of us standing on the stairs were not sure what we were looking at. This person looked like she had been dragged to the ranch from the back of a chuck wagon after a cattle drive. We looked at each other and no one had any answers. The Colonel pushed her way through the circle of onlookers with Chop following close behind. He pushed his way to the front, knelt down on one knee, and took the woman's dirt caked wrist in his hand. He had done this with many of us who had taken sick to see what we were dealing with. He could tell exactly what the problem was and how it needed to be treated with his herbs. The Colonel told us that he was feeling for the blood pumping through her body.

After what seemed like forever, he stood up and spoke to the Colonel, "She is exhausted and needs rest for now. Then we will find out her story."

We hauled her into one of the smaller rooms by the kitchen so Chop could tend to her, which was no easy thing. She was not a small woman and stank to high Heaven. I guessed a good wash was the first order of business but I did not want to be the first in line to sign up for the job.

A couple of hours later I headed down stairs after my "packing" was finished to see what kind of progress was being made on the stranger. Two of the girls were cleaning up the mess of linens and water with rolled up sleeves. I never thought I'd be happy to have the excuse of getting ready for the trip. The Colonel was standing at the foot of the bed with her arms crossed.

"You know Cisco, you'd think I've seen just about everything until another one of these gals shows up on my door. It's amazing to me what people do to themselves and each other."

I looked down at the woman's newly washed face. She was a black woman, probably escaping some kind of horrible situation. I could tell by looking at her that she was once pretty but life sorta beat it out of her. She seemed to be pale, shaky, and restless. She started mumbling. We had to lean in to get her words.

"You see. I found it Mam, I sees it, one mo step, one.."

I shot a confused look toward the Colonel. "What do you thinks wrong with her? Is she sick?"

"What you're lookin' at Cisco is the effects of *laudanum*. We found it in her pocket." She pointed toward the bedside table and sure enough, there was a little bottle that read:

Oleander's Tonic

Women's Tincture
A cure for restlessness and
all female malady.

"This kind of *medicine* has the nasty habit of doing more harm than good. Best you get on up stairs now and bring down your bags. I want to meet with you and Book before you go on to the train. This one'll live, which is not in her favor right about now."

*

The woman's eyelids twitched. Ghostly visions passed through her brain. Laughing faces with long teeth chased her bare legged figure through the shadows. It was like a never ending nightmare that kept on going from one horror to the next. In one scene her mother was hanging from a tree and swinging back a forth, in another, her small brother reached for her, "Don't you leave me!" their fingers barely touching, and then he was gone. She was running through the madness trying to come back, laughter all around her, and a menacing voice that told her, "You'll never make it. You belong to me."

Her eyelids fluttered open. She almost wished they hadn't. Her body shook and her lungs felt like they were trying to breath under a pile of rocks. She reached up and touched her forehead. Definitely clammy, just like she felt. She took a look around trying not to move her head too much. She was in a clean room, washing stand, bed, and chair. Just as her eyes lit on the door, in bumped the biggest Chinaman she ever saw carrying a tray.

"Good Lord help! I've gone done died and ended up in the bad place."

"You might just think so young woman before I am done with you. For now, you will drink this tea until I tell you to stop."

Her eyes searched around the room frantically and landed on the bedside table.

Lee glared at her knowing what she was searching for, "It's gone. You'll take no more of it while you are in this house. Now sip this tea, it came all the way from the Tianmu Mountain in China just to help you."

She tried to sit up but dizziness took her and she dropped back onto the pillow. Lee put the tray down and helped her up to take her first sip into the land of the living. It was all uphill.

5

D, Book, and I met with the Colonel in the parlor for serious conversation about our upcoming travels.

"Now Cisco, I'll have Chop give you gals a ride to the train station in the wagon. I know you like to ride yourself but I want you to really think about what train travel might do to that horse of yours. With all the bangin' and bumpin' around and strange surroundings, who's to say what kind of trauma he will have. What if something happens to him? This outfit wouldn't be much without him."

This idea tore at me. First the danger about Book and now I couldn't even take my own horse. We go way back! I call him The Red. My devil of a dead father rode him around like a prize which he won in a card game with a fine southern gentleman. We been through hell since we rode off in the night away from our burning homestead. Still, I knew in my heart that what the Colonel said was true. The rails were no place for an animal with no experience. We built this place on The Red. I hung my head and nodded. The Colonel reached over and put her hand on my shoulder.

"You're a good hand Cisco. Have I ever told you that?" I turned to look at the Colonel and noticed there was a little water filling up so I looked away.

*

We were standin' out on the front porch with a small crowd of well-wishers waiting for the wagon to be brought around when we heard a shout coming from inside. All our heads turned in the direction of the commotion just as the Colonel came busting out. She was wiping her hands on a rag and cursing a string of words that I won't repeat. It's not a good idea to be in the way when the Colonel gets heated up. It's kind of like a steam train haulin' right toward you with the face of a bull. She had her cigar clenched in her gritted teeth. When she opened her mouth we all ducked to get out of the line of fire.

"Someone bring me my Dragoon so I can plug myself in the head and put myself out of my misery! Chop! You hurry on now with these gals and get back here before I up and kill this gal while we get her clean from the Miss!"

The Colonel swung the door back open almost ripping it off the hinges and heaved it back closed with a bang that shook the walls. We heard yellin' inside again. I took to helping Chop heap our bags in the back of the wagon out of sheer nervousness. I leaned in and whispered to him, "What's this *Miss* she needs to clean up? I thought she was washed when she got here."

"The *Miss* is what we call laudanum. Have you ever heard of opium? That woman in there is suffering from withdrawal symptoms. Her body has grown used to the drug and needs it to function. Don't look so worried, we have dealt with this kind of thing before. She will survive the laudanum but she may not survive the Colonel. It is best if I take you and come back as soon as possible. Are you ready for your departure?"

I took a look around the group on the porch. All of them leaning away from the door and jumping every time they heard the Colonel yell. I knew I would miss every one of 'em. D was standing there, a little dressed down with her "finery" packed up. She still wore the split skirt with a red button up shirt tucked in. Her tall hat sat back on her head, making her spray of freckles stand out even more. She had a smile playing at the corners of her lips. Book stood next to her with one elbow on the wagon. She had on men's pants with a yellow faded men's button up shirt tucked in. She had her hair trimmed shorter under her hat and a red kerchief tied around her neck. I put on almost the same outfit except the shirt was brown. No particular reason I spose, I just liked brown.

I turned to Chop. "Well Leon! (That was short for Lee On) I don't see how we can leave at any better time." We rode away from the Flying Bird with the sorrowful glances of those wishing they were leaving with us. For the moment, I didn't blame 'em one bit.

6

Our little town was one of the lucky ones that ended up being alongside the tracks of the great Union Pacific. Some towns that were passed up just rolled over and died off. I wondered who bribed who to get ours on the map. New buildings were being put up every day so that I hardly recognized it. We could hear the train coming in the distance when we paid for our tickets. While I read mine, D leaned in and explained that "Way" travelers were going one way and we were to travel second class. This bit of news was no shock to me as figured I traveled this way most of my life. Chop pulled up the wagon so we could untie D's gelding and she set out to get him to his stock car safely. Her horse had traveled this way before and didn't seem bothered by all the activity. I missed The Red but was glad of my decision before long. The noise! The stock door banged open, then banged closed. There was shouting and clanking and any number of other unidentifiable commotions.

"Well gals! We're set! You ready?" D strode up to us with an air of confidence and her trademark grin.

We all said our goodbyes to Chop. I patted his huge shoulder. "Well Leon, don't forget to duck."

"No worries, I have had more practice than any of you. Speaking of duck, I wonder if you can see a friend of mine in Omaha. The young woman at the ranch who I am treating needs something that I am running out of. The information is all here, along with payment."

He handed me a folded note and small pouch of coins. The note read: See Lung Hay-Chinese Herbalist at Duck's Dry Goods for Fog tea. Kindest regards, –Lee On

*

We were soon bumping along the tracks. The conductor came by to punch our tickets and gave a look at Book but said nothing. I was soon watching the land roll by outside. I was so tranced I forgot about my fellow travelers. The sound of page turnin' going on next to me helped me to remember. It was my good friend and riding partner Book. She was holding, well, a book. I'm tellin' ya she was holding it right up to her face so that I asked myself, "Who reads like that?" I watched her for a minute and broke in just when she was about to turn another page and whip it up close again.

"Lemme take a look at what you're reading there."

"Oh yes, a very interesting little book I picked up from the news butcher on the way in."

I closed it up and looked at the cover. "Adventures of Buffalo Bill, from Boyhood to Manhood; say, haven't you had enough *adventure* already without reading this stuff!" I read on, "Maddened with fright, the bull rounded into the air, exhorted wildly, gored those in advance, and soon led the herd." Who talks like this anyhow?

D was all of a sudden paying attention with a slight grin which I ignored. Book grabbed the "book" back and said, "For your information, this is called a dime novel and I find it to be a good read as do many other people."

"Well, if I were you, I wouldn't believe anything they write in those rags. They're for children and fools."

D butt right in, "You never know Cisco. Someone just might take to writin' bout you some day. You better hope you don't run into Ned Buntline." There was that grin again!

"Well, let the record show that you can count me out on that deal my friend! I ain't no attention seeker and that's for sure! Dime novels! Buffalo Bill! Ned Buntline! I'm goin' for a walk!"

When I walked away, they still had their sappy grins on. It took me a few steps to get used to walking on the train as it rumbled down the tracks. As I headed down the aisle toward the front of our car I really started to get a good look around. Cornelius! We were a cramped bunch of sorry travelers. We had every kind of person crammed all together, cowhands, farmers, miners, hunters, families with children crying. And let me tell ya, things weren't smellin' like a rose neither! There was a mix of tobacco smoke, dust, and humans that didn't know the meaning of the word soap. At least I was able to stretch my aching backside a little. Some toothless old boy spit out his tobacco and barley missed my toe. I gave him what I call a lead-filled look and he just smiled at me with his stained beard and two remaining teeth. I needed air!

There was a small standing space between the cars that had someone in it. I cursed my luck and noticed the young man in the space was not much older than myself and moved as if he was goin' to throw himself under the train! I jumped forward and grabbed the back of his shirt, barely keeping him from falling. I set my feet and yanked with all my might. Hearing the rip of his shirt, we both fell backwards with my head dangling over the side. I saw the tracks racing by over my head and squeezed my eyes shut. I could feel my head snapping up toward the train as he grabbed for my shirt to pull me back up. I heard the rip of own shirt and was soon leaning against the wood of the car trying to breathe without throwing up whatever breakfast I had at the ranch. My hat was popped back on my head and the young man crouched down in front of me. His face slowly came into focus. Golden brown hair and light mustache. Those eyes! Bright blue-green. He was shaking my shoulder gently.

"You all right? Hey!"

"Me?! Just what is it you thought *you* were doin'?! You could've taken out the both of us!"

We just sat there staring at each other until his eyes moved down to the middle of my shirt. I looked down to see what he was looking at. Two or three of the buttons were torn clear and my bandages were showing through. Now, if I might back up a tick, I can tell you that I had kept up my men's outfit by wrapping up my already small chest. I don't have time to tell ya the whole tale right now; I had a bigger problem on my hands. I held my breath and waited for him to give me away. I knew that he knew what was up by the look in his eye. The wheels were turning.

He finally said, "Well, that must have been one mean bronc to have broke up your ribs up like that." He gently reached up with a sparkle in his eyes, flashed me a set of dimples, and closed my shirt together.

I yanked my hand up and grabbed my shirt closed. I was angry that my cover had been blown. I didn't know this character or what he would do with my secret. I asked, "What's the idea!? Why were you cashin' in your chips?"

He sat down grim faced and ran his hand through his wavy hair. He held his hat between his hands and told me the tale of how he lost all of his money to a cardsharp on the train. He was traveling back to Omaha after selling some land his family gave him.

"It was all the money I had in the wide world. I was gonna save it for a ranch of my own someday. Now I have nothing, no one. My family is gone; I figured I may as well be too. My pa always said I would never be nothin', looks to me like he was right." He looked sorrowful out toward the passing prairie. I knew how he felt at that minute. The heat was rising in my face and that old anger was flaring when I finally spoke up.

"We're takin' you back to your seat. I'm gonna change this shirt and come back to get you. I wanna see this cardsharp fella you're talking about. What's your name anyhow?"

"The name's Guthrie, but my friend's call me Jigsaw." He sparkled those eyes at me again.

*

I was back at my seat after he was back at his. My two traveling partners were gaping wide-eye fashion at my appearance. I strapped on my holster and grabbed another shirt, brown again, out of one of my bags. I stomped off without a word toward the back of our car and to the "retiring room." This one needs an explanation. To make it simple, you have two spots to relieve yourself at the back of a train car. The only thing separating you from the others is a curtain. The man next to me was having a little trouble "retiring." You could tell by the sound coming through the curtain. I was glad I only had to change my shirt and was soon adjusting my holster while making a beeline for Guthrie and his card trouble.

"That's a honey of a pair of smoke wagons you're carryin' there." He assessed my guns up and down with a grin.

"Colt Thunderers from my Ma. Don't ask. Best thing for you to do is stay on the back side of 'em."

He smiled even bigger now. "Well now, I'm right glad for the warnin'."

He showed me to the place where the cardsharp was dealing. As we came upon the spot I felt a little confused. Sitting there was an elegant lady in a large hat. She had on a black velvet skirt and short jacket with fancy embroidery all around the edges. Her lace gloves daintily shuffled the card deck. Her hair was black as night and kind of pulled back in a delicate web of a braid. Around her neck was a fine lace scarf held by a oval black pin. I could smell some kind of flower which I knew wasn't coming from *anywhere* else.

I swung around to Guthrie and he nodded. I wasn't countin' on this but I wasn't about to back down neither. She stopped shuffling and her wide brimmed black hat turned in my direction. Her eyes were black like the rest of her clothing. I couldn't tell if I was looking at someone living or not. Her small face was perfect. Small nose, small rose bud mouth, smooth pale skin. She was like a China doll I once saw in a window of a shop. She smiled up at me and her eyes fluttered with long black lashes. She had a sing-song voice that made me feel edgy.

"You know, I just knew I had company. Would you like to play?" She looked past me at Guthrie and smiled.

I sat down and tried to look for a sign of life in those eyes. No dice. She dealt the cards and we were in about two hands with me losing bad. One the third go, I happened to notice the slightest flash coming from her lace sleeve while she thought I wasn't looking. I threw my cards down and grabbed her wrist with one hand and pointed my gun in her direction with the other. We stared at each other. With those lifeless eyes fluttering she tried to pull her hand back. I twisted it as hard as I could and cards started to flutter to the floor. All aces.

"I believe this pot belongs to my friend." I clenched my jaw and tried not to pull the trigger.

"Who the devil do you think you are?" Her voice wasn't so sing-song anymore.

"How ya doin' here Cisco!?"

A quick recognition came over the sharp's face when she heard my name. Word gets around in the West if you make a name for yourself, and it usually sticks. I once shot down a famous outlaw; maybe she figured she was next. She quickly recovered and smiled sweetly at D who had come up behind us with the conductor.

"Well now, your friend has had a streak of luck." She pushed the pot toward me with her dainty gloves.

The conductor blew up. "Alice! I thought I told you about sharpin' on this train! If I so much as catch you flippin' one card before our next stop, I'll flip you from outta my train while it's still movin,' ya hear!" He turned to me. "How much did she skim ya for, son?"

"I figure she's about all paid up. Ain't that right ma'am?" She gave me a slight upturn of her perfect rose bud mouth and nod of her hat.

7

We were back in our seats and relating our story to a wide-eyed Book.

D pointed in my direction and said, "Ya see, I told you I had to keep and eye on this one."

"Listen here, D. If you're smart, you won't mention that again." They both looked at each other with those sappy grins again.

I was saved by the train whistle and the conductor yelling that we had our first stop. The train slowed and jolted to a stop in a place that was not much more than some thrown up shacks and a dining hall.

"Twenty minutes! Eat if you're hungry!"

Doors were thrown open and people rushed out like the train was on fire. How they expected us to get ourselves fed and back on the train in that time puzzled me. We were finally sitting down with our meal of beefsteak, fried eggs, and fried potato. I had a chance to look around. We were a crowd of ragged, dusty, men, women, and children. There was an especially sorry group passing us that D leaned over and told me were emigrant third class passengers. Some had painted marks on their wrists. The marks were mercury that they used to paint on to keep the bugs away.

I was thinking how glad I was to be in with second class when the cardsharp in black floated past. She gave me a dead-eyed glare and lifted her lace hand to her hat. She swished into a waiting carriage and then was gone.

"I want to thank you for that."

I turned around to see Guthrie standing behind me. He was looking toward the dust where the carriage had been. My eyes went to where he was looking.

"Don't worry; you had about as much chance against that one as a snowball in a hot oven." I turned back around to see him give me a sparkle and I felt a heat rise up in my face.

*

We were soon crammed into our car and rumbling down the tracks again. There was endless space as far as I could see, above and below. The land stretched on until it touched the blue skirt of the cloudless sky. We hadn't caught sight of any buffalo yet. I knew that Book was keeping an eye out for them but I didn't say anything. I figured that they were being wiped out along with the lives of her people. The thought made me fretful. No one had said a word yet to Book. I took Keyes to the side before we left the ranch and explained my little plan of having her trim Book's hair real short this time. I thought maybe somehow folks might take her for being from Mexico. Of course I didn't figure out what would happen when someone tried to speak to her in that language. One thing at a time.

D's voice broke through my thoughts. "Hey Cisco, that Guthrie fella ain't half bad."

She raised one eyebrow and waited. I could feel my face getting hot again and Book staring a hole through the side of my head.

I pulled my hat down over my eyes and said, "I don't have time for that kinda talk. Bring it up once more and see what happens."

*

Some might think that train travel is a good way to see the West. Those are the ones who travel in the first class Pullman cars. Believe me, I tried to take a little stroll on up there and got told to go back to my seat. We saw a couple first class travelers who strolled through our car to get an idea of what was goin' on our way. They hurried back to the front of the train with dainty hankies over their noses and sour looks on their faces. I had to admit the rank air was increasing at a fast clip. So far our "trip" was about as refreshing as being burned at the stake.

The news butcher stomped through every now and again with an endless supply of goods for sale; newspapers, books, candy, cigars, sundries, you name it. They were even selling a plank of wood to set up between the benches to make a bed. We were told that we needed to "buddie up" for the night. That meant we could sleep two to a board. It seemed that there was no end to the discomfort. The benches barley fit my backside and it was hard to take after a while. Sleepin' on 'em seemed an even worse idea.

We stopped a few more times and meals were mostly the same. You had to check your watch to tell which meal it was; breakfast, dinner, supper, all the same. You had a fine choice; beef steak, fried eggs, fried potato, that's it. One time we got excited over "chicken stew" that turned out to be prairie dog! Still we rushed out, if only to get a break from the cramped car. I never saw first class rush out because they got fed in their own private cars. Who wanted to know what they were eating? I didn't. It would only add to the misery.

By now we were getting to where we were going. The end of the tracks was Omaha. A few were sick with various ailments; headache, sore throat, influenza, stomach ache, and all manner of general grumpiness.

The gas lamps were lit at night and I wondered to myself if we would become one long, burning worm of flame into the night. The conductor came through to help us buddie up to sleep. Book and I were together and D was matched up with a nice older woman traveling alone. I was hoping that the woman was the snoring type!

I closed my eyes to sleep with a smile on my face. One seat over the sound of snoring was going off like charges of dynamite. Maybe Book was right. There was a God in Heaven.

8

"Next stop, Omaha!" It was like music to my ears. We were chuggin' alongside the Missouri River heading into town. I was just about to dance a jig when I got slammed from the side and almost knocked to the floor. I pointed my gun and Book gripped my arm. By now I learned to trust her judgment on certain things.

"Don't do it." She whispered into my face. "This man will kill us and he is not alone. The dark one is with him."

I searched her face for an explanation and I followed her eyes to where the man was thrashing his way toward the front of the car. All I saw at first was a big buffalo hide robe with a dusty black hat on top. Behind him rushed a smell of death and sweat like a river. My stomach felt sick. He swung back around like he felt our eyes on him. He studied my gun. Have you ever seen someone that makes you wonder "What am I lookin' at? Is it an animal or a person?" It was like the human was swallowed up into some kind of beast. He had pale yellow eyes. Kinda like a wolf. His hair was shaggy, grimy, and tangled. His mouth broke into a jagged sort of grin. It felt like he was hunting us and he knew we had no escape. His yellow eyes locked into mine and then he turned and kept going.

I all of a sudden realized that I stopped breathing. I looked over to Book who was whispering something to herself. The train whistle screamed, making me jump and cutting through the moment like a knife. I could feel the wheels slowing down as we headed toward town.

*

We got off the train and tried to swat the ashy dust from our clothing like so many others, only to find it had dug its way into everything we carried or had on. I hated myself and trains about now. D had gone on to get her horse and we looked around to see a large banner on the side of the station that read, "Welcome Buffalo Bill!"

"Look at that, Book. That's..." As I pointed, Book had her eyes squinted up and was walking toward the sign like she was trying to get a better look. She was walking out into the middle of the street when the sound of horses came pounding around the corner just missing her. I grabbed at her arm and yanked her back.

Someone yelled at me, "What's that Mexican kid trying to do, get hisself killed!"

Book looked around trying to figure out who the Mexican kid was while I yelled back, "He's no concern of yours!" She looked at me like I was crazy.

"Who is that man talking about? What boy?"

"Never mind that! What in Pike's name do you think you are doing walking about in the street!?"

She looked confused, mumbled, and rubbed her eyes. "I couldn't see it."

"See what!?"

"The sign."

We sat down and waited for D to come back so we could plan out our next move. It was getting darker now and I could see clouds coming in overhead, bringin' with 'em an angry rumble. I was tryin' to figure what to do about Book. I remembered how she was holding that dime novel on the train so close and now the sign she couldn't read. Maybe she needed a doctor but we didn't know anyone. I realized then as I looked about that Omaha was a big, busy, dirty place. A dust devil whirled past us carrying sand, pebbles, and all kinds of trash. We covered our faces with our kerchiefs and our eyes with our hands. I heard a window break somewhere.

I figured we could ask around and have someone point us toward Chinatown to Duck's Dry Good's so I could pick up the package for Leon. This made me think of the Flyin' Bird Ranch and I was shortly wishing we were headed home.

My eyes were traveling up and down the dirty street; General Dry Goods, Lean Agent, Hardware, Drug Store, Newspaper, Dressmaking, Restaurant, Bakery, Saloon, Saloon, Ice Cream Parlor, *Ice Cream Parlor*?

"Hey there Cisco! See ya round Omaha!" Guthrie tipped his hat as he walked down the street with his smile and totin' his saddle over his shoulder.

I pushed my hat back and rubbed my dusty forehead where a pounding of dull pain had started. I heard the sound of D's voice break through my closed eyelids.

"Well we're right as mail! What do ya say we head out!"

She had the gelding saddled up and our bags strapped to his back. She looked sprite as ever with her grin lighting up the whole street. I looked over at Book who was starting to get up.

"Hold up a tick D. We have to get ourselves pointed toward Chinatown to pick up that medicine for Chop. Another thing.." I looked over at Book who was presently squinting at horses and people passing by. I said in a low voice, "Do you know of a doc or somebody who can take a look at our friend's eyes?" I made a point motion with my finger in Book's direction. D followed my finger and her eyes got big as plates.

"I had a wonder 'bout that." She threw her thumb in Book's direction. "Sure. We can go by Vincent's place. He's a brother to a friend of mine at the Wild West. I bet he could fix us right up."

We followed D down a couple of smaller streets and through the shouting, laughing, and shooting, we could hear a faint sound of music floating toward us. It was leading us to a storefront.

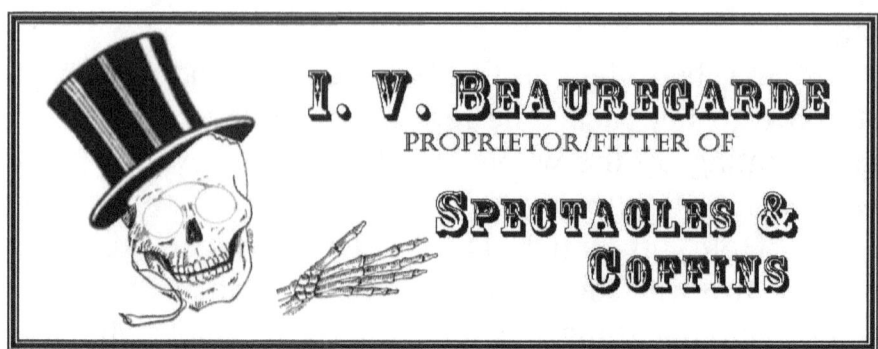

We could hear the strange music clearer now. There was a crack of lightening that lit up the sign followed by more rumbling. We could also hear a man shouting something from inside.

D looked over at our wide-eyed faces and kind of laughed. "C'mon pards, don't get shy on me now."

9

We looked down through the storefront windows and saw men's and women's fancy clothes hanging there. When we went into the shop I could see that hanging below where the pants and skirts should be there was only a long black cloth. My eyes traveled around the room and landed on a long table with candles flickering all around a casket. The room smelled funny like flowers and medicine. We looked at each other took a step toward the table. There was a sign above it that read:

We have roamed and loved 'mid the bowers,
When thy downy cheeks were in their bloom;
Now I stand alone 'mid the flowers,
While they mingle their perfumes o'er thy tomb.

D whispered, "Say, this one looks pretty good. Almost like he was livin' or somethin'."

In the casket lay a stringy looking man with a puffy red nose. His greasy black hair was pasted to one side. He had his long, bony fingers folded across his chest. They were holding a fresh white flower under his pointed chin. There was a rank odor of alcohol on him.

I don't think any of us saw someone dead up that close so we just stood there frozen like. All of a sudden the lids of his eyes began to flutter. I can say for sure that we all took a jump backward at this new development. The dead man sat straight up and looked around with eyes peeled open. He looked down at the flower and flung it across the room. His scream started small like steam building up in a tea pot. Soon it was at a full whistle and the stricken man leaped out and passed us in a flash. The black cloth around his waist caught in the door and hung there as the only sign left of him. He ran off pantless into the night.

We all just stood there gripping each other's shirts for dear life. D said, "Now that there's a crepe hanger!"

There was a faint sound of footsteps behind us and a deep voice that said, "Splendid timing, gentlemen!"

We whipped around to see a medium tall young man. His dark hair hung to his shoulders and swung over one eye. He had a sly smile on his oval shaped face and as I looked down over his clothes I could tell they were pretty fancy at one time. They fit perfectly but were tattered at the knees and elbows. He wore all black except for his lace collared white shirt that was unbuttoned a little and sort of hung to the side. I couldn't see his whole face but I could tell he was handsome in a strange sort of way. He shuffled his black buckled shoes again toward us and looked at the black cloth stuck in the door. He turned and grinned again at us with his slight chin beard.

"I lose more display models that way. Onward! Goldie, my dear you look ravishing as always!" He took D's hand, brought it to his lips and produced a red rose from behind his back. He placed it gently into her hat and swung toward me and Book.

He then grabbed the strangest pocket watch out and took a look. I could see the metal wheels turning inside of it. "Welcome to Farnam street, gentlemen, and like I said, splendid timing indeed! Shall we?"

He pocketed the watch and led the way with a sweep of his hand and a swish of his lace cuff. We walked past a display of caskets of all kinds: pine, painted, polished; some even had little windows on the top. He led us to another room that he called his study. I never saw any place like it.

He had books stacked against the walls in every direction. In the middle of the room was a polished wooden desk that looked like it was made for a giant. On the desk were all kinds of glass bottles filled with different colored liquids. Some had little animals and bugs floating in them. Some were being heated by little flame burners and bubbled quietly. There, sitting on the edge of the desk, was some kind of moving machine that looked like a clock. The metal wheels were turning and steam was puffing out of one side and up into the air. I saw another long table with all sorts of shiny instruments that I didn't ask about. I figured that had to do with the undertaking business and I was still a little shook from what just happened in the other room. On the walls where there was space he had displays of strange flying bugs in frames. Some were skeletons of small animals.

I was wondering what D had gotten us into now when he sat us all down and began to play his violin. The music floated around the gloomy study. Just as quick as he started, he stopped and held out one of his hands toward us. The candles flickered around the room.

Lightening from outside flashed. Vincent held his hand up toward the roof and burst out in a booming voice,

"Thou wast that all to me, love,
For which my soul did pine-
A green isle in the sea, love,
A fountain and a shrine,
All wreathed with fairy fruits and flowers;
And all the flowers were mine.

Ah, dream too bright to last!
Ah, starry hope, that didst arise,
But to be overcast!
A voice from out the future cries......."

"Onward!" This was a creaky voice calling out from a dark corner of the room.

All of our heads whipped in the direction of the voice. From out of the darkness came a flying thing, black with wings flapping. We ducked and I felt the swoosh of wings blow dust from my hat. The black bird landed with a thunk, grabbing his perch on the big desk, and looking around the group.

Book looked at the bird and said, "Kangee, we meet again." Another flash of light came from the front of the store followed by an angry rumble and the patter of rain hitting the roof.

Vincent pointed his finger at the bird and shouted, "Must you interrupt with your unsolicited endings Edgar!? These gentlemen were being a very kind audience to my performance! Your theatre critique skills have been well noted and cast askew. I was delighted at having another opinion!"

"Hah!" The bird croaked.

Vincent glared at the bird, "Gentlemen, I would like to express my sincere apologies. We have no right to be merry at your expense. Hello! Edgar!"

At this point I was getting sort of impatient and cut in, "Look here, Ivy. Do you know anything about eyes? *Goldie* here tells us you might." I looked over at D who was staring all dreamy like at Vincent.

"Ain't he a pretty talker Cisco?"

"Yeah, well, talk is one thing. No offense, mister, but we came here on business. You see my friend Book has been having trouble reading." I thumbed in Book's direction and she gave me an 'I'm gonna shoot you with an arrow when we get outta here' sorta look.

Vincent and the bird stared a hole through the middle of my head and I started to squirm in my seat. I thought I might have angered him because he didn't move or answer for so long.

He yelled out and I jumped. "Magnificent! Return to the beginning, Frisco my friend! Am I amiss! Did you say Ivy?"

I returned his stare, "That's short for I.V. I didn't get the first name."

"I like it! What say you, Edgar!?

The black bird blinked at me.

"The *I*, my friend, is short for ILLUSTRIOUS! Fitting, don't you think?" He gave a wink to D who smiled back. "And now for your friend... what may I call you?" He reached out and took hold of Book's hand, giving it a firm shake.

"My name is Talking Book. When I was a young girl it was Talking Bird. My grandmother gave it to me after seeing me talking with Kangee." She made a motion toward the raven that ruffled his wings and settled back down.

"You mean to say that you had a conversation with a raven? Extraordinary! They are the most intelligent of birds, complete with even larger egos. But how did you learn to speak so well, my friend. Your grasp of the English language is quite impressive, I must say."

Book smiled, "I was sent to live with missionaries for some time."

"What an adventure you've had!"

I cut in with my best smart-alec tone, "That's what I keep telling her." She kept looking straight forward.

"Hello! Let's see if you might need spectacles. Do you know anything about the optick sciences?"

He may as well have been talking to us in Chinese words. He looked around the group of wide eyes and open mouths.

*

He threw open a drawer in his big desk and pulled out a long stick that he swung around like a sword. He walked over to the wall, reached up and pulled on a string. A chart unrolled to show drawings of eyes and writings with arrows pointing to different parts. He whipped his pointing stick up in the air with a swish and tapped the chart.

"Now then! Newton wrote: 'Are not gross Bodies and Light convertible into one another…and may not bodies receive much of their Activity from the Particles of Light which enter their Composition?' What of the Frictional Electrostatic Generator? No! No one!?"

He looked again around the group of wide eyes and open mouths.

"Gentlemen, I am a practitioner of vision science serving my apprenticeship in London. Simplified…if I must, I am a fitter of glasses or *spectacles*."

Edgar flapped his wings and croaked, "Proceed, Ivy!"

Victor whipped the pointer toward the bird and shouted, "Silence! You devilish antagonist! Talking Book, if you will be so kind as to step over to my examination chair?"

Book was soon sitting in a sort of tallish barber chair. Vincent had an ink pen with a long flowing feather on one end and was slowly moving it back and forth. He told her to follow it with her eyes.

"Hmmm....well." He walked over to the chart on the wall and pulled down another string. This one had large letters all in lines that got smaller toward the bottom. He started up again, "This is called a Snellen chart, my friends. It tells me how well you can see. Would you be so kind as to tell me what it is you do see, Talking Book?"

She squinted up her eyes and read as much as she could. Pretty soon she closed her eyes and rubbed them with her dusty hand.

I was feeling bad for her because of the fretful look on her face. I cut in, "Ok, so what goes on? Can ya tell us the trouble or not?"

Vincent was throwing open another drawer and took out a polished wooden box. He unlatched and lifted the top. It was hinged so that three more drawers came out with the first one. He then reached to tie his hair back with a black ribbon he took out from one of the drawers. Looking back and forth, he spotted what he was looking for, and walked over to Book. In his hand was a metal device with several round glass pieces. He held them up to her eye one by one until she opened her eyes wide.

"My goodness!" was all she said.

"Precisely my friend! Now, I think that I might have what you need."

Next he opened a cabinet with all different kinds of spectacles hanging and in drawers. He mumbled to himself and finally we heard, "Ah ha!"

"We can thank J. Bausch from Germany for these little gems. What do you think? They are made from hardened rubber, quite durable indeed. Give them a try!"

He fastened them to her face and around her ears and took a step back. They were small and round but looked nice on her face. She gripped the sides of the chair and opened her eyes wide. She looked back and forth across the room and jumped up toward the chart on the wall. She read every letter all the way down to the bottom. She lifted the spectacles gently up to take her shirt sleeve and wipe the muddy tears that made a puddle there.

I reached into my money pouch and looked at Vincent who stood there smiling at Book. "What do we owe you Ivy? I'd like to thank you for helping my friend."

He looked at me and a large grin spread over his tiny beard. "Nonsense, Frisco! I won't hear of it! You have all been of great company to me and that is payment enough. Why, I'm surrounded by barbarous fools at all times and you were quite a welcome respite. A glorious diversion, if you will! Let me know if you require further assistance in *either* of my fields of expertise."

This reminded me of the pantless man. "What was all that business in your parlor? You know, the display model?" I pointed out toward the front of the shop.

He thought for a minute and smiled again. "Oh yes, I have a running agreement with a group of gentlemen who call themselves the Casket Club. I allow them a little game of cards every week in my parlor. If anyone drinks himself into unconsciousness, rather than having the fellow lie about, I set him up as a display model until he comes to. This makes for an awful shock I imagine. It is my stern advice to stay away from the game of Monte in Omaha." D cut me a look.

He walked us out with Edgar sitting on his arm and pointed to the piece of black cloth still swinging in the doorway. "As you can see, some of my top notch casket models have windows on the top half. The lower half is insignificant, therefore unnecessary. It's better than fashion, is it not?"

I stood there thinking how I wouldn't want to be buried with my lower half covered in black cloth, while Book walked around examining everything like she never used her eyes before.

It seemed that the thunder storm had passed by leaving huge puddles to the sides of the road. We thanked Vincent and headed out with directions to Chinatown and Duck's Dry Goods. He called after us, "Lung Hay! Splendid Herbalist! Give him my greetings! One more thing," he said to Book. "You may do well to make a visit to Julius Meyer. He will be able to answer some of your questions. He has a curious emporium called the Wigwam!"

I couldn't help but wonder how Vincent knew that my good friend and riding partner needed some questions answered about her family. I kept it to myself and she had a smile on her face. I passed over it for now.

10

Coming into Chinatown was grim. It was muddy and hard to find our way in the dark once we got off the main street called Leavenworth. We started to pass opium dens. They had a sweet smell and so much smoke you could barely see the flicker of lit candles. Leon told me once that opium came overseas with the Chinese but that the English brought it to China from India. It was used to even out the trade for tea that the English bought so much of. I don't really care where it came from. As far as I knew it sure wrecked a lot of lives. I thought about that gal back at the ranch.

The Chinese had names for alleys like we have for streets. The one we were looking for was called "ya hu tong" or "duck alley." D's gelding started to get a little jumpy. I had to admit I felt it too.

I elbowed Book. "I don't like this place Book. You gettin' anything?" She just looked around like she was waiting for something.

We passed a few more dim alleys. I didn't turn my head to look into them for fear something might pop on out. Our footsteps echoed out into the dark ahead of us. D's horse stopped short and wouldn't go any farther. His ears were cocked ahead and you could see the white around his eyes. If you weren't sure what you were in for, it was always a good idea to look at your horses ears. They knew trouble.

"Say, I don't like this. He don't wanna budge and that ain't good." D talked softly to her horse and patted his shoulder. "That's a good pard. We'll get ya outta here soon."

Out of darkness glared a set of yellow eyes. Just like the ones I saw on the train. I reached for both my guns this time. D's horse backed up and snorted. We heard a deep growling sound that made the hair on my arms stand up and my stomach sick. I was one click away from pulling the trigger when we heard a shout from behind us. The person was using angry Chinese. D's horse reared and we all turned our eyes to see a small boy holding a lit torch. He was motioning us with his other hand to come with him. I looked back to see that the yellow eyes had disappeared.

He came toward us whispering loudly in Pidgin English, "You come with me now! It's no safe for you here!"

"Hold up a tick, how do we know *you're* safe! What was all that yellin' about? What was that thing after us?" I pointed back toward the darkness where the eyes were. I could feel my heart still pounding.

"That is chai ren. Now you must come!" He looked behind us with fear in his eyes.

D cut in, "Where ya gonna take us? How do ya know who we are?"

Book tapped my arm, "I think he is safe but we must leave now, away from this place. The boy is right."

The boy nodded his head up and down, "I take you to Doc Hay. You know, Doc Lung Hay?"

I looked over to D who gave me a shrug of her shoulders and we set off after the boy into a maze of more alleys. There were small shacks, vegetable gardens like ours at the ranch, a loud gambling hall with shouting, and a temple they call a "joss" house were I could see candles lit and glowing incense sticks with smoke curling toward the roof. We came to a row of particularly shabby shacks with flickering lights in the windows. I could see shadows moving inside and stopped to get a better look. There were all sorts of men walking up and down the small street. I could hear rough laughter and someone screamed. The boy ran back with his torch and grabbed my arm.

"That the row. Bad place for girls. We keep going, we almost there now."

*

The boy fanned out his tiny hand. "You see, Doc Hay."

Right in front of us was a large pond. All around the outside were the dark shapes of sleeping ducks with heads tucked under one wing. There was a small wood bridge that went over the pond lit by burning torches. It led to the storefront of Duck's Dry Goods. Inside was a glow that I was happy to see in all the gloom that surrounded us. The small red door opened with a jingle of bells and out came a smiling Chinese man. We had a shock when we saw he dressed just like us. He was wearing pants with six guns strapped to his hips.

He walked toward us over the bridge and spoke to us in perfect English, "As a rule, I find horses bothersome and expensive animals so I don't own one. If you look to the side of the store, you will find a small corral where you can keep yours. It should be quite safe as most of my countrymen feel the same way as I do." He held out his hand toward the boy. "I see you've met Shih-shao."

*

Duck's Dry Goods was a well organized little store with shelves filled with all manner of things. I handed the note to Doc Hay and had a look around. I saw boxes of soap, tobacco, candies, razors, canned goods, books, clothing, and other sundries. Above the shelves I spotted a sign that read:

"Annual income twenty pounds, annual expenditure, nineteen six, result happiness."

–Charles Dickens

He had a nice little wood stove glowing in the corner and a table for eating. Eating! My stomach just let me know that there was the most delicious smell of food cooking somewhere. The other two had caught a whiff and were looking around to see where it was coming from.

"I was concerned as to the fate of my old friend Lee. It is not so safe for Chinese these days. I am glad to find that he is well and glad to meet some of his friends." He held out his hand and gave each of us a shake.

"Well, we were sure glad to meet your boy when we did. He jumped in and saved our skins from something he called chai ren." I pointed toward the wide-eyed little boy.

Doc Hay looked fretful and turned toward the boy who only nodded his head up and down. They spoke in Chinese to each other and the Doc soon turned back to us. He was thinkin' hard before he said anything. We were all real quiet and waited for him.

"The Chinese believe in evil spirits. These are sometimes animal spirits who take the form of humans. The boy is speaking of chai ren or "wolf man." Can you tell me if you have seen anything strange in your travels?"

I gave out a little laugh. I could have handed this man a list as long as the tracks of the Union Pacific of the "strange" things we saw so far! Then, I thought of the man on the train who almost knocked me over.

"Come to think of it Doc, there was this man with yellow eyes." I gave the Doc an account of our travels up to the present.

"The Chinese believe these spirits avoid light. I try to keep the store lit up at night so my countrymen will find comfort here. Please be my guests. I have a tub for washing and enough for you to eat. I will fill Lee's order for you to take. I suggest that you stay the night with me and set out in the morning. Shih-shao can show you the way to Julius Meyer. He is not far from here."

"How about you, Doc, what do you think about this 'wolf man'?" I asked him the question that was lingering on all our minds.

"I have my traditions. I also have my six guns." He smiled and patted his holsters.

11

"Quack! Quack! Quack! Splash!"

The ducks woke me up. There was a beam of light coming through a bamboo shade and hitting my eyelids. I felt better after a little clean up and some food in my stomach. We ate the most delicious noodles with vegetables and broth. I must have fell asleep pretty quick because I don't remember even lying down. I looked around the back room where our bedrolls were and mine was the only one still rolled out. It was a tidy little room with a trunk and small bed. Under the bed was a line up of strange shoes. Then I heard talking in the next room.

I entered the room with my friends smiling up at me. Book looked up with her new spectacles and syrup in the corners of her mouth. She pointed to her plate and said happily, "Hotcakes!"

After the clean-up, we were getting ready to head out and Doc was in a little caged off area where he kept his drawers of herbs. Something was boiling in a pot on his cook stove that smelled kinda like flowers. He had a bag he was filling with Leon's order.

"You must give Lee my note and these." He held out two books one by one and read them to me before putting them in the bag. "Teachings of Confucius, and Oliver Twist by Charles Dickens. I think he will enjoy the last one immensely."

I looked at the note but couldn't read it. It was written in Chinese.

"Have Lee read it to you. It will be good practice for him." He smiled and handed me the bag.

"One thing, Doc, I was wondering how your boy knew about us coming. How'd he know where to find us?"

"There are many eyes and ears around Omaha. You three were not hard to find. Shih-shao is my helper, not my son. His mother died in what we call 'The Row' or the place of prostitution. Many Chinese girls are sold from their families to 'work' in Tie Fow, the 'Big City' of San Francisco, or in other places. Most find their way into slavery and death. I try to help them the best way I can. Sometimes it is not enough."

I looked around to my friends. We all knew exactly what he was talking about. It seemed liked there were slaves of all kinds in our day.

I held out my hand to the Doc, "Thank you for everything. I wish I could say that I'd come and see you again, but I doubt it if I have to ride that old train one more time."

He gave a nod of his head, "You should take the trip in the third class car if you want real adventure."

"No thanks Doc! I've no need to have mercury painted wrists. The only adventure I'm looking forward to is sleepin' on the trip home."

*

We headed out of Chinatown with Shih-shao in the lead. He was a quick little devil and we had to walk fast to keep up with him. Pretty soon we were back on Farnam Street in front of another store called the Wigwam.

He fanned out his little hand again and smiled, "You see, Julius Meyer." He then gave a little bow and took off to who knows where. We were left looking at the sign.

INDIAN WIGWAM

JULIUS MEYER 163

There was a note on the door that listed some of the goods: Julius Meyer Interpreter - Purveyor of Chinese, Japanese, and Indian curiosities, cigars, tobacco.

Curiosities just about covered it. D stayed outside and fussed with her horse. Book pushed the door open first and we just stood there looking around the room. There were so many things it was hard to take it all in at one glance over. There were all manner of things hanging from the walls; most of them looked Indian made. He had Chinese type vases and statues, a thing that looked like a crazy red and yellow monster with whiskers that was made of paper, fireworks, Indian rugs, a buffalo robe, you name it. There was a long counter made of glass that had things displayed in it like bundles of arrows, dried herbs, hatchets, baskets with colorful designs, tobacco, pipes of all sizes and shapes, and small Indian dolls with colorful clothing and beads. I walked over to look at a few pictures that hung on the wall and called Book over. We didn't see the "purveyor" yet, he must have been in the back.

"Hey Book, you know any of these fellas?"

She adjusted her glasses and looked at the pictures of groups of Indians sitting out in front of the store. You could see a white man standing in the middle of the bunch who must have been Julius Meyer. He had a small, dark mustache, smaller chin beard, dark wavy hair.

Book whispered something to herself, "Tsitsistas."

I guessed it meant something in her language. Right after, the head of a man popped out from behind one of the shelves and we both nearly jumped out of our boots.

"Your people? Is that what you said, "Our people?" He came walking over toward Book who had a look of shock on her face.

She said softly, "Yes. I have not seen them in a long time."

"Yes, well there has been quite a bit of trouble for them, what with the buffalo hunts. I am saddened myself, many have become my friends. My name is Julius, and may I say that you speak English very well." He held out his hand. "How may I call you?"

"I am Talking Book, this is my friend Cisco." He looked me over and then smiled, "It is a pleasure to meet you. Is there anything I might help you with? I speak the language of six tribes so far. Go ahead and try me out." He smiled and crossed his arms.

Book let go with both barrels. I guess she had a lot built up to say and it felt better to say it in her language. They went back and forth with Julius looking very serious and listening when she talked. I liked this fella. He seemed to actually care about what she was saying; only interrupting to ask a short question or give an answer. Book listened to him and then finally looked down at her boots, shuffling them, and nodding her head sadly.

He finally spoke up in English, "Well, I've heard that many of them are traveling with the Wild West. At least they can keep their customs and freedom while they remain with the program. The government has given Bill Cody charge of them and he is said to treat them decently."

"Well Jules, it just so happens that we are headed over there and who knows what we might find, right Book?" I looked at her and patted her shoulder, trying to say it a little cheerful so she would feel better.

He caught on to what I was trying to do and chimed in, "Well of course! I've heard rumors of quite a few renegades out there who you just might run into."

His little dark mustache and chin beard turned up and he gave me a wink. Like I said, I liked this fella.

12

"We're burnin' daylight gents!" D was standing outside and smiling up at us.

We headed to the outskirts of town and came over a small ridge. Laid out below us was a giant meadow with a tent city of people and animals. I could see movement everywhere I looked. There were people moving, guns popping, horses running kicking up dust, and there right in front of us grazed a small herd of buffalo. Someone was shouting and it made an echo and seemed to come from everywhere at once.

I whistled and said to myself, "Lord Amighty."

"Nahsir! That there's Bill's Wild West." D's eyes sparkled as she looked out over the meadow.

*

She led us down a trail and toward the giant camp. The smell reached us before the camp did. I could recognize animals and food cooking but there were other things floating up that I had no idea about. Book's eyes never left the herd of buffalo. We passed by a game that was being played in another open area. One cowboy hit a ball into the air with a big stick. He ran around the group touching stuffed sacks with his one foot. Other players tried to throw the ball faster than the runner, finally one that caught it tried to touch him with it. There was smiling all around and yelling for the next hitter who came up and swung the stick back and forth waiting for the ball to be thrown. Book and I were at a loss.

I tugged on D's shirt sleeve and pointed toward the game, "Say, D, what's the deal with that goin' on over there?"

"Hey, ya'll gotta remember one thing around here and that's the name they gave me is Goldie. Don't ask me why and I don't give a care as long as I got work. Haven't you two ever saw a baseball game?"

Book and I were at a loss again.

"You all sure don't get out much! They say that there's gonna be our national game. Come on, we need to get settled and then I'll give ya the tour."

There seemed to be a sort of main street between the tents and all manner of traffic that included people and animals. We came to a tent and stopped with D holding up her hand.

"Now hold on and let me go in and check to see if anyone's dressin'. The way you two look, you could cause a stir." She winked and disappeared.

We could hear laughing from inside and a yell came from D saying, "All clear! Come on in!"

There were a few bunks and a trunk or two with gear spillin' out. A girl sat atop a bunk with her elbows resting on her knees and her hands dangling between 'em. She had on a getup that was like D's the first time I saw her ride over the hill to the ranch.

She also had on a smile that was as big as her hat with an even bigger bow that tied back her mass of red curly hair. She jumped up to shake our hands.

D did the intro, "Cisco, Book, this here's the Desert Rose, but we all call her Texas."

"Howdy!" She pumped our hands and smiled with her green eyes. She had a pretty oval shape face and rosy cheeks. A tiny splash of freckles sprinkled all around it.

Book and I nodded and I took a look down her outfit again. She had a split skirt and a vest with beaded stars . Around the bottom of the skirt was some kind of wavy feathers that I couldn't figure out.

She laughed and told me, "You're lookin' at a gen-u-ine fashion victim of Queen Veloria! Well, see ya 'round. Hey Goldie! You all better snap it up or you won't be ready. You don't want to make Nate cross." She looked at us and smiled again like she had a little secret and I was beginning to wonder if D had told her too much. She said, "I hope ya'll like our little piece of Heaven!"

We waved and I thought to myself that I hoped Heaven didn't look anything like what I'd seen so far or no one would want to go there.

"Well let's get our stuff tucked in here. We'll figure out later where you two will bunk for the night. We can't have two boys bunkin' in with us respectable types." She laughed at her own joke.

"Hey D, I hope you are bein' careful about what you tell on with me and Book. We don't know who we can trust."

"Don't you get your worries up now, Cisco. Your secret's safe with me. Now come on and help me get our bags in here. Pard needs a break and he's gonna need a good rub down after that trip."

We headed out toward the horse and I looked over at Book hoping D was right about keepin' our secret safe.

*

A pack of dogs ran through the streets of Omaha. Some of them might have been pets at one time only to be cast off and left to breed uncontrollably. They mostly ate the garbage that people threw around, but once in a while attacked farm animals or even people if they got hungry or brave enough. They crept up behind a buffalo robe in an alley. The alpha dog went out first baring his teeth in a challenge. A low growl rumbled around the pack. The buffalo robe turned and stood to its full height, flashing its yellow eyes.

The alpha cowered and tucked his tail. This was a bad sign to the rest of the pack. There was a yelp and the pack took off in retreat.

The yellow eyes of the predator shifted back and forth searching for more challengers. There were none.

13

"Now those tents over yonder belong to the cowboys." D pointed them out. "You know, I heard some one say they were gonna give us the name 'cowboy *girls*'. It's all entertainment I figure."

"Does that girl sharpshooter bunk in with you?" I wondered since I didn't see anybody but the Texas gal.

"Oh no, we all don't mix much. Bill has her set up special with her own place. Here we have our social tent." She waved toward a large tent with an open front. We could see movement inside, but right about the time we were gonna step in, some cowboy flew past us while being thrown out. Cards were flying in a cloud around him through the air. I grabbed out my gun lightning quick and pulled off two shots. Just reflex I guess. Everyone around us stopped and stared. One man picked up one of the cards I shot at. He made a low whistle.

"Eewwee, look at that! Ace of clubs. Hole went right through the club!"

Some one else waved him off and said, "Come on now, that ain't too special. We got a girl around here that does that!"

There was laughing and then it was back to business. I heard a laugh I recognized coming from behind me and turned to see Guthrie standing there with his grin sparkling. Heat came to my face and I gave him a lead-filled look. He just waved and kept walking.

I turned to D, "You didn't tell me *he* worked here."
I thumbed in the direction Guthrie went.

She grinned at me, "How did I know you were interested. You told me not to bring it up again, remember?"

*

Ned Buntline walked over to pick up the other card the young man shot at. It was an ace of diamonds. The hole went right through the diamond. He smiled to himself, tucked the card into his vest pocket, and followed the three into the tent.

*

We stood there watching some kind of game being played by two men hitting a ball of string back and forth over a stack of books in the middle of a table. They were using cigar box lids to hit the ball.

D leaned in and said, "Don't tell me, ya'all never saw table tennis."

I looked at Book and then back to D, "We don't get out much."

D slapped her leg and laughed, "Cisco Peach, you're a wonderment!"

A deep voice cut in. "It would be my pleasure to buy you refreshments."

We turned to see a mustached man walk up from behind us. He was wearing a rounded hat and a buckskin jacket with fringe. He smiled and held out his hand. "Welcome to the Wild West, my name is Ned Buntline. And you must be the famous Cisco Peach that I have heard so much about on my travels. May I buy you a drink?"

I looked down at his hand and then into his eyes. I could see he had dollar signs where his pupils (I learned that word from Vincent) should be. The way he looked made me feel mean. I figured I was just another dollar sign to him.

"No thanks Ned. I don't drink, that goes for my friend here too." I thumbed toward Book.

He held out his hand toward Book and smiled, "You must be Talking Book. I have heard a great deal about you as well. You sure you wouldn't like to sit down awhile? I might have a business offer for you both. After all, it was I who created Buffalo Bill and you can see where that has gotten him." He waved his hand around like he built the place with his own two hands.

To my surprise, it was Book who spoke up. "Thank you for the offer, Mr. Buntline, but my friend and I are not interested in stories. We have had enough real *adventure* to last a lifetime."

We left him standing there with his mouth hanging open and continued on with our tour of the camp.

D pointed up toward a small ridge where there were a group of teepees. They were set aside on their own with smoke curling up and out the top. Book just stood there frozen in place.

I put my hand on her shoulder, "Ya see, old Jules was right, let's go on up there and take a look around."

"You all can go take a look, I have to get back to the tent and get ready. You two stay out of trouble and don't forget to watch the 'ex-hibition', Bill don't like it called a show. I'll meet ya back at the tent right after."

She walked off and we headed toward the teepees. We followed a sign that read, "Indian Village" with an arrow pointing the way.

There were mostly women and children in the village. Some were cooking, some were cleaning, and one was working on a brightly colored blanket she was weaving on a frame of wood. Book seemed to be searching for something she couldn't find. She reached up her fingers, pushed her spectacles up, and rubbed her eyes.

I tried to help her, "I have a feeling this ain't all of um Book. There's probably more somewhere else."

She nodded her head and we turned to leave when I felt a tug at my shirt. We turned to see a pretty woman standing in back of a little girl. The woman held up her hand to Book and began to tell her with her hands that the men were down getting ready for the 'show'. Book said something back with her hands and we left with hopes to find the rest.

"Say, you're pretty good with that hand thing." I told her. She smiled back at me.

14

Coming down the hill we could already hear the sounds of the crowd and the music. We were getting close to the area behind the big curtain. There was a powerful loudness all around us and we nearly got killed when a line of charging horses ran past us through the opening side of the curtain.

"Ladies and Gentlemen! Welcome to the Wild West, Rocky Mountain, and Prairie Exhibiton!"

We watched as the line went past and into the 'exhibition'; Indians in war paint, Mexicans, men in beards with funny hats, all manner of people on horses. Then, there was D and Texas, a couple others and the cowboys after that. People were clapping and cheering and the music was playing.

"Let us welcome now, that Illustrious Monarch of Showmanship, the Prince of the Pistoleers, Buffalo Bill Cody!" The crowd went wild.

There was a blur of a white horse and buckskin racing past, and we decided to try and get around the side of the curtain to get a look at what went on. We found a spot between the curtain and the seats and squeezed in to watch.

We saw a line up of all the riders in a big square with Bill Cody out in front. Some of the riders held stars and stripes flags up high while they fluttered in the prairie breeze.

He held his hand up to the crowd, "Ladies and gentlemen permit me to introduce to you a Congress of the Roughriders of the World!"

His horse pawed up at the air with his front hooves. The crowd went wild again, clapping and waving their hats and paper programs.

"Now if you will join me as we sing *The Star Spangled Banner* in honor of this great nation, The United States of America!"

The band struck up with the song and people stood up all around. The men took their hats off and put them over their chests. Soon everyone was singing along and feeling pretty proud about it. I looked around the crowd humming to myself until my eyes lit on an Indian warrior. He sat on top of his black and white pony in all his war paint and feathers. He looked straight ahead and wasn't singing. I remembered Book and looked at her standing next to me the same way. I felt sorrowful then. Memories floated past my mind while the music played; the buffalo hunt we passed on the trail, D tellin' us about the Indian Village, her face after she talked with Julius Meyer. I pushed my arm up and around her shoulders and we just stood there like that.

The song ended, the white horse reared again and he was gone. The riders raced around the arena, more clapping and waving. A girl raced into the ring atop a brown and white horse.

"Ladies and gentleman welcome our very own Peerless Wing and Rifle Shot! Miss Annie Oakley!"

A cowboy rode in with her and started throwing glass balls into the air for her to shoot. She hit every one.

Some men raced in carrying a table with guns laid out on it. She leaped off her horse heading for the table and jumped clean over the top, grabbing her weapon when she did. More glass balls were thrown into the air and blowing apart. I heard some woman scream next to us but there was mostly a loud roar of clapping and yelling. Then next thing she did surprised me. She picked up a knife from the table and used it to look over her shoulder. Pointing over her other shoulder with her rifle, she shot at a card a man was holding up for her. He held it up toward the crowd showing the hole went clean through the spade on the ace.

There was more yellin' as she bowed to the crowd, jumped up on her horse and rode out. Buffalo Bill stood by the opening and we heard him say, "Sharp shooting Missy!"

Book leaned over to me and said, "I've seen better." She smiled and patted me on the shoulder.

"Well, I don't know about that. Maybe we can practice that knife trick back at the ranch. You can hold the card." I winked at her and she shook her head in a "Not a chance" fashion. Then we heard the beating of drums.

*

They seemed to come from everywhere at once. We held our breath and waited. My heart was beating along with 'em.

"Ladies and gentlemen, for the first time seen in any American production and exclusive to the Wild West Exhibition, may I present to you, SITTING BULL!"

A spotted pony rode into the ring and stopped. Women fanned their faces and gasped. He sat there with his chin high wearin' long braids and looking over the crowd. The drums stopped and singing could be heard from behind the curtain in his own language.

Book whispered, "Tatanka-Iyotanka."

I leaned toward her, "He one of yours?"

"No, I have heard many stories of him but have never seen him."

He lifted up his buckskin sleeve in a wave as he rode around the arena. The crowd broke into a roar again. There were about twenty warriors that came in after him and rode around wildly and followed him out again.

Just about then I noticed some kid gnawin' on a corn cob wrapped in paper and remembered the pancakes we ate so long ago for breakfast in Chinatown.

"Hey Book, what do ya say we scare up some grub? All this ridin' and whoopin' around is making me hungry."

She agreed and we set out in search of the said grub.

15

You know they had a whole outfit of cooks makin' food. We were soon sitting happy with plates of beans and roasted chicken in front of us. The biscuits tasted *almost* as good as home. We were finishing up and heading back when Book felt a hand on her shoulder. She turned around to see a full feathered warrior standing there. He didn't say anything but gently reached up under her hat and felt around the edges of her cut hair with the back of his hand. He moved down to trace her glasses. I could tell something powerful was happening. He had a sort of sad look in his eyes and they stood there for a long time just starin' at each other.

Book reached up and put her hand on his shoulder and smiled. They talked for a minute in their language and I got the feeling that they knew each other. When they were done, he reached out his hand for me to grab.

"Cisco, I would like you to meet my friend Looking Glass."

He looked at me and gripped my hand real tight. His hand felt strong and his skin felt warm and rough. He had the most beautiful honey brown eyes with a light ring of gold around the brown. He looked over at Book, said something in her language, and then turned toward the sound of the noisy crowd. He lifted his hand and disappeared around the corner.

Book followed him with her eyes until he was gone.

"Looking Glass told me he had to go attack a settler's cabin. We will talk later. Do you know what he could be talking about?"

"Well Book, only one way to find out. Let's get back to our spot and see what goes on."

*

We stood there and watched as the woman in a sun bonnet yelled out the window of the little square wooden building. She was throwin' her hands up in the air and bawlin' "HELP!" Warriors were whooping and running their horses around the "cabin" shooting arrows. The music got louder; the dust got thicker and in rode the white horse with Buffalo Bill to save the day. We saw Looking Glass pass us and give a wink. He was a fine looking young man a little older than Book. He rode off with his red war paint striped cheeks and feathers flyin'. They cleared up the area and rolled off the "cabin" on wheels.

"And now, ladies and gentlemen! Give a grand welcome to our Lady Wrangler of the Plains! Goldie riding Blackjack!"

A rearing black horse bust upon the scene. It dove through the air, ducked its head, and threw its hind end up like it was gonna kick the lid off the place. She was right. They loved her. She hung on like a tick and waved her hat while the horse tried it's best to rid himself of the rider. Pretty soon a cowboy rode in and up next to her and she grabbed his shoulder and pulled herself aboard. Two more cowboys rode in and roped the wild horse. We ran around back to get a look at D. We were almost rundown again, this time by some men fighting to get another rider aboard an angry grey horse who was havin' none of it. The rider was thrown clean of the mess and lay on the ground holding his head. It was Guthrie.

Bill Cody stomped up to the group, "Hold 'em there boys! Have we no other rider to take this young man's place!?"

The man on the horn yelled, "And now! The Wild West would like to present Jigsaw Guthrie riding Hailstorm!"

Everyone jerked their heads toward the arena. Poor Guthrie looked miserable. I cannot give an account for my next action. I can only say that I wasn't thinkin' very clear. I waved my hand at the men and handed my guns to Book. I felt hands grabbin' at me and was thrown up and on the storm deck of Hail the angry horse.

Cheers of the crowd faded in and out. One of my hands was flung wild-like into the air. My bones crashed so hard on that animal's back that I thought I would be pounded into powder. My hat was flung somewhere. My only thought was to just hang on because I knew if any part of my body connected with the dirt I was gone for good.

I saw the cowboy ride in out of the corner of my eye. I reached for him and took a jump for the back of his saddle. Hailstorm saw what I was about to do and reared, taking me with him. Everything got real quiet. I could see myself flying through the air in slow motion, then nothing.

*

It was like tryin' to see from under water. Shadows were moving around me. Noise and voices floated in and out. I could hear Book and D. I could feel someone patting my face with something.

"Hey now Cisco, you come on back to us." I could hear D saying.

I tried to open my eyes up. I could see someone had lit a lamp. My head felt tight like it was trying to grow and had no room. Man, I hurt all over. Book's face came in and out of view with the blinking of my eyes. I reached up my hand to give a wave.

"I bet that old Hailstorm is just about broke by now. Cause I know I am."

D said, "You rode 'em slick and that's a fact! That's what we call it when you ride without tying stirrups like us gals. You rode 'em slick, like the boys do!"

My two friends had a good laugh and I tried to sit up. I noticed my chest felt tight and looked down at a set of new bandages that were wrapped around my middle. I felt them with my hand and looked quickly around D's tent. Book and D knew what I was thinking.

I gritted my teeth, "Where's that doc?"

16

They both had their hands on me, trying to push me back down.

"Book! Talk some sense into er. Cisco you can't just jump up and go lookin' for the doc. He says you're to stay put!"

"I tell ya if you don't let me go, you'll both be sorry."

A sharp pain came up through my ribs and slapped me back down onto the cot. I grabbed for my side and tried to get up again.

"Cisco, look at me! Don't you trust me?" Book was looking me square in the eyes. "Don't you trust even me?"

This question threw me off. I sat there and thought about it. Did I trust anyone? I ran away from people all my life till I came to the ranch, people who I didn't trust. Maybe I was still running in my head. Where did that leave my good friend and riding partner? I put my head in my hands. My head hurt something fearful.

"My head."

"I know Cisco, I know." Book patted my shoulder.

The flap of the tent was flung back and in walked Bill Cody.

"How is our patient coming along Goldie girl?"

"Cisco just woke up sir, as ornery as ever." She wrinkled up her freckles in my direction.

I peeked out from under my fingers because it got quiet. I saw him standing there in his tall boots and buckskin.

He leaned down in my direction and lowered his voice to almost a whisper, "I have consulted with our camp doctor and I am thankful that you were not more seriously injured. You are a brave young woman and I am in your debt. You will always have a place in the Wild West if you should so desire."

My heart took a skip. The man said "young woman." I felt done in. I guess he could see it on my face because he spoke up.

"Your friend Book has told me of your wish to remain in disguise. Have no fear. I myself know how important appearances are. I have sworn our friend, the doctor, to secrecy with the threat of unemployment and certain ruin should he let on to your true identity. Like I said, I am in your debt. However, should you change your mind; you have only to lift your little finger. I could make you a star." He gave me a wink and held out his hand.

I reached up for it and got a good stab of pain for my trouble. I thought about joinin' the West for a tick but then all the faces of the girls back at the ranch flashed in front of me. The Colonel's words came to me. "Did I ever tell you you're a good hand Cisco?" I was needed back at home, *my* home.

"I'll thank you kindly, Bill, but I'm needed back at the ranch."

*

There was a stampede down the slope leading to the meadow. The small herd of buffalo and elk were restless and could not be quieted. Two cowboys headed them off before they ran into camp.

"What's wrong with 'em Buck? I never saw 'em this riled."

The six foot cowboy reined in his horse and sat up tall in the saddle looking around in the dusk shadows for a clue.

"Search me Kid. There ain't been many wolves in these parts since the elk got hunted off but you never can tell. Maybe our animals are drawin' 'em in. You keep an eye out and I'll get a couple of extra hands for tonight."

"Ok Buck, just what I need is a pair uh yella eyes lookin' out from the dark about now!"

*

I was finally standing and walking about slowly with Book and D on both sides to help me. I wouldn't take a drink for the pain. I hated whisky and I saw what laudanum did to the girl at the ranch. I just had a broke rib or two. Getting' back to town might be a problem so we decided to wait and stay the night. We headed out for the Indian camp in search of Looking Glass.

A soft glow and wild piano music was comin' from inside a tent we were passing. D gave a little laugh and we looked at her to explain.

"That, my friends is the tent of our Queen Veloria. You remember Texas and her feather outfit?" I read a wood sign with fancy writing hanging in the front of the tent. It read: Veloria Beauregarde – Purveyor of the fabulous in high-toned fashions!

All of a sudden the tent flap was swiped back. There stood a curvy woman with dark hair piled high wearing a black and purple corset. She had feathers hanging around her neck and sparkly jewelry hanging from every which way. A large white smile stretched in the middle of her caramel colored cheeks. She had a spark of devilment in her eyes.

"Did I hear someone mention my name?"

D gave a little wave, "How do, Veloria?"

"Yes and how does our Lady Wrangler of the Plains. One thinks you do very well doesn't one? Now cut the crap and come on in for something cold, all *three* of ya!"

We got introduced and stepped into the tent. I was glad to have a seat for a spell and took a look around. She had two big red velvet cushion chairs with golden silk pillows. I could see the small piano she had in one corner lit up with candles. Hanging from the roof was a twinkling sky of Chinese lanterns. She had hanging racks of costumes of all colors, some with feathers, and some with fringe. There was a large round mirror that hung in one corner, under it a long table with all kinds of fancy bottles. Two tall chairs sat next to each other waiting for the next "fashion victim" I guessed. Then I noticed something strange.

Lined up right next to each other on the table were wooden forms that looked like human heads. On top of the forms sat what looked like a scalped pieces of gold and silver wavy hair. I just kept staring and thinkin' what poor soul was running around with a bald spot where her hair used to be.

Veloria came up next to me and handed me a cold drink from her ice box. She leaned on my shoulder and pointed at the wooden heads, "Not everyone knows that the famous Bill Cody wears a hair piece."

I looked at her. She raised one of her eyebrows and took a drink. I could smell her perfume float around my head. It smelled like being in the trees with the sun breaking through the leaves and a flower here or there. I liked it because it wasn't sweet. She took a drag from her long cigarette holder and blew it up into the lanterns.

"Sandalwood from India. It reminds me of the Empress Victoria and her son." She pointed to a picture of a bearded man in a gold frame.

"What is her son's name?" I asked. We were both still looking at the picture sitting on the piano.

"Prince Edward, my fashion savior, of course." She looked around to the others, "Did you like my music? It is called ragtime. Someday it will be all the rage."

D cut in, "I ain't ever heard of that kind of music before."

"Of course not, and do you know why? Because in this tent we do not follow trends, we create them!

We all nodded and tasted our drinks. I never tasted anything like it; it was kinda sweet but with a bite.

She smiled, "Root beer. It's better than fashion, don't you think? I don't drink alcohol."

Something about what she just said was familiar, like I heard it somewhere before. She took a look at Book and threw her hand up in air.

"Ahh, I see you've been to see my brother!" She framed Book's face in the air with her hands.

D and I looked over at Book.

"They are perfect for your face."

Her skirt made a ruffling noise as she swung over toward Book. I say swung because she had a way of swinging her hips from side to side as she moved. She traced the bottom of Book's hair with her finger.

"May I ask who the devil cuts your beautiful black hair?" She put one hand on her hip and pointed back ward toward me. "I'll wager it's the same one who cuts our little *outlaw* in the other corner." One of her eyebrows shot up. "Now my dears, if you want to put on a distinctive persona, you must practice good grooming techniques."

We both started to make up a story but she held up her hand and then clapped both of them twice. A small animal shot out from the corner of the room, jumped onto the piano, then leaped onto her shoulder. I was so shocked I nearly spit out my drink.

17

"Kiddo, tell these ladies who they are dealing with."

The small brown monkey held both of his tiny hands over his mouth and made a laughing noise.

"Let me introduce myself." She swept her hand in the air and brought it down in front of her. "Ms. Veloria Beauregarde, at your service."

D said smiling, "She's Vincent's sister."

"Yes, but Vin is a bit more of the dramatique. Now will you allow me to trim up those señors and shape your cuts just a tad?" Her shapely eyebrow shot up again waiting for an answer.

I don't know about Book but I barely heard what she was saying because I was staring at her monkey. I never saw one before. He looked like a little brown, furry, old man. He had on a purple velvet vest with black trim and a tiny black round topped hat. We both must have been staring because she figured we weren't paying attention and told us the tale, of the monkey that is.

"I sprung him from Barnum's show. I didn't want him to fall victim to shoddy entertainment, of course. The Wild West is higher-toned than a mere circus. Am I right Kiddo?"

He reached up with his tiny hand, lifted his hat, smiled and put the hat back down on his old man head.

I suddenly remembered the word "cut" and looked around to see the "señors" she was talking about.

She was one fast and smooth talker. Next thing ya know we were in the chairs and I heard the snip snip of cutting going on all around us. She had every kind of cutting tool, brushes, powders, and perfumes on her table.

She talked the whole time she was snipping, "Now don't you two think twice about me giving you up. Lean back. Discretion is part of my job here. Some day there will be more women such as myself breaking into barbering and I plan to kick open the door for them. Sit up straight. I think of myself more as a stylist of sorts. Do you think I would get anywhere by flapping secrets of my clientele all over camp. Why Bill would run me out! Hold still now! Like I was saying, my gads, you have such thick hair. Drag that lamp closer will ya Goldie? Bring me another of those root beers. Can't you see I'm working? Is it hot in here?"

I heard her open a can and felt her spread something on my hair. I recognized the smell right away and looked up. She whipped me around toward the mirror and showed me myself. She held up a can of Cisco Peach men's hair pomade and smiled.

"Courtesy of Cisco Peach, fabulous, am I right?

I looked at the familiar can and it took me back to the General Store where it all started. The man at the counter asking me a list of questions, me seeing the advertisement for Cisco Peach pomade on the wall, blurting out that my name was Cisco Peach, the shot I took at the gunman, me running. It all seemed so long past. I stared at my reflection. You know, I liked it.

*

I eased up and out of my chair to take a look at Book. Both of our cuts were close and curved around our face real nice, the front was swept up and out of the way without the choppy look we were used to. She handed me a set of cutters for Keyes to keep up our new "look." I tried to give her some money, but she pushed me off.

"Nonsense! I heard about what you did for Guthrie today. That is enough payment for me and it was my pleasure! I'm off with the show to England next and to meet Edward. Maybe I can get my hands on a few of those crown jewels." She winked at us.

Someone rushed up to the tent and yelled in, "Hey V! Bill needs you right quick and says it's a matter of an urgent nature!"

"Every matter with that man is of urgent nature! Tell him I'll be right along!"

She grabbed up her small carpet bag and started throwing all kinds of her little bottles and brushes inside, talking all the time.

"Sometimes that man gives me a headache. Have you seen my shears? What do I put myself through this for? Hand me that bottle please. I should just stay in England and visit with my family. Now let's see, I shouldn't forget that, excuse me please. Kiddo let's go!

Where is that little heathen? I could just squeeze him to death I love him so much!"

She flung her black feathers around her neck and the monkey jumped up on her shoulder and lifted his hat.

I suddenly thought of the señors, "What about the señors you were trimming?"

"Those are the little hairs sticking out around the bottom, of course. Gotta run, fashion calls!"

She swung off with a wave. I could still smell her perfume. I stuffed the cutters into my belt and off we went again to the Indian camp, our trail lit by the lanterns of so many tents.

18

Shadows from the fire danced on the sides of the teepees. The smell of wood smoke floated by, curling up and into the starry sky. I could see the flames flicker in the reflection of Books spectacles as she listened to Looking Glass talk. There was group of us sitting all around the main fire at the Indian camp listening to tales of time before the settlers came to the West. Some spoke in broken up English, some with their hands, those that spoke in the same language talked to each other. I watched a young child in his mother's lap batting away quietly at the fringe and beads of her buckskin dress.

D leaned in, "Is that there a friend of hers?"

"Yeah, I'm pretty sure they go way back. I been waitin' on her to tell me about it."

We sat staring into the crackling fire. It felt kinda peaceful sittin' there in that camp. Earlier we ate a little of their meat and flattened bread that was offered to us. My ribs still hurt powerful bad, but the food helped me to get my strength up again. Book brought me some god-awful tasting concoction to drink and I drank it down without complaint. Afterward it kind of made me feel warm and a little tired. I was glad to be standing, that gray could have kicked my head in! That made me think of Guthrie. I wanted to ask about him and how he was doing. The thought of it made my face red and heart heavy till I was disgusted with myself and quit thinking about it.

I was brought out of my thoughts by a short gust of wind that fanned the fire sideways with a whoosh. I thought somebody was walking by the fire. I looked up and froze. There, cast upon the side of a teepee was the black shadow outline of a wolf. Its teeth were bared and I heard a low rumbling growl. My stomach felt sick remembering the train and what happened in the alleys of Chinatown. The wolf man was back! I looked around wildly thinking I would see those yellow eyes peering out from the dark. My eyes stopped at Book who was standing with her hand outstretched in the direction of the shadow.

The woman held her child in close and two of the men reached for their weapons. D and I reached for our guns. The teeth snapped and the growl got louder.

Book was whispering something to herself and suddenly yelled out, "Silence! Be gone!"

The sound of her voice sent a chill down my back. A rifle shot rang out from down in the meadow, followed by shouting. It was too far away and I couldn't figure what they were saying. The wolf shadow let out a yelp and we could see it run across the teepees in retreat. Then it disappeared into the darkness. We were left holding our weapons on the teepees with the quiet crackle of the fire. Everyone was looking around for an explanation.

"No Nehe."

"Sunkmanitu Tanka."

"Skiri."

Three people answered at once in three different languages.

Book looked over her shoulder and said, "Heavohe." She had a very serious look on her face and spoke with a strong voice. It was like I was seeing her for the first time. She was the daughter of a chief. My good friend and riding partner was a princess.

The face of an old man came floating up into the firelight. He had the lines of many years and many battles scratched on his face. His eyes were steady as he looked around the group. His long black and silver hair was expertly braided on each side. He spoke to one of the younger men in his language and I could tell he was questioning him about the recent goings on.

The same man turned to us and spoke in English, "Sitting Bull would like to know, what is this talk of devils and wolves and the sound of rifles?"

Book lifted her chin and said, "Tell Sitting Bull it was Maheo, the Great One who has protected us from harm."

There was more talk between the two men.

The younger man spoke again, "Sitting Bull says that the wolf has always been a friend to us and that harming him will bring harm to our people."

"Tell him no wolf has been harmed and he does not need to fear for his people. Tell him that the Great Spirit will deal with all Wakanpi in his own time."

At the word Wakanpi, Sitting Bull raised his eyebrows. He spoke to the man one more time.

"Sitting Bull would like to know why the Wakanpi listens to you."

"Tell him it was because he saw the Great Spirit standing behind me."

When Book said this, every single person looked behind her. I for one didn't see a thing but if she woulda said that wolf heard the Great Spirit speaking outta her mouth and lit out, I wouldn't have argued one peep.

Sitting Bull stared at her and she stared right back. No one moved. He finally nodded his head and was gone without a sound.

We returned to our fire and were told by a messenger of Sitting Bull that we were invited to stay the night in the camp. D was tickled that this solved her problem of where to put her hat wearin' friends. She said goodnight to us and headed down to her tent and to get news of the shooting we heard earlier.

*

"I swear, Buck, I thought we had a wolf in camp!

"Don't fret Kid, you didn't shoot the man on purpose. Why just look at him, he don't even look human with that raggedy hair and coat. How was you to know?"

"I wonder what he was headin' for up in that Indian camp, Buck? Creepin' along quiet like he was huntin'. It was those eyes that flashed at me in the dark, like they was afire or somethin'. Look at 'em now! Why theys as plain as you or me. I coulda swore they was

90

yella. He smells like dead hide. What if he was one of them Wendigos! I hear they eat people!"

"No matter, he ain't goin' nowhere now. You hang here and look after the stock. I'll go tell Bill."

*

Everyone had turned in except for three of us who sat around the fire.

"Hey Book, what was all those words you used a while back? I couldn't hardly keep up."

Looking Glass answered first and I was surprised that his English was pretty good.

He said, "Some at first said it was a wolf. Talking Bird told us that it was Maheo or Creator God who protected us from a Wakanpi or bad spirit."

Book cut in, "Looking Glass is right. I am also surprised that Sitting Bull invited us to stay."

"I'm kinda glad he did, Book. I don't mind it up here. What do you think Looking Glass? Come to think of it, how do you like this whole Wild West business, with all that runnin' around the wagons and whatnot?"

He looked into the fire and sorta smiled, "Some say that it is a bad thing for us to travel with the Wild West. I can only say that for me, it is better than staying on the reservation or running. I travel and see many things. I get paid and have a chance to teach others of our ways. Soon we will travel across the water to meet Grandmother England."

"Yea, I know what you mean about runnin', I did that most of my life. I sure am glad I met our friend here though." I patted Book's shoulder.

Book looked at Looking Glass, "Do you remember when I was sent away with the gun traders? It was Cisco who rescued me from them."

He looked at her with his eyes tearing up, "I can never forget the day when you were taken away." He looked at me, "I am forever in your debt and hope you will call me friend also."

I wasn't sure what to say so I just held out my hand to him. He took it and gripped it hard.

Book smiled, "Looking Glass and I were children together. I taught him how to speak English when I came back from the missionaries."

"That explains a lot," I said. "I'm hopin' you'll visit us at the ranch someday, Looking Glass."

They both looked at each other and laughed. I was finally let in on their little joke.

"He is one of a few who have kept watch on our ranch many times. Remember the deal I had with my father? He joined the Wild West when the rest went to the reservation."

"Well then." I waved him off with my hand. "You sure ain't gonna need any directions from me."

We all started laughing then.

*

Later Book and I were looking up at a circle of starry sky through the top of a teepee. We were both on our backs with our hands behind our heads.

"You know Book, that Looking Glass fella ain't half bad."

"I don't have time for that kinda talk, bring it up once more and see what happens."

I smiled to myself and fell into one of the best night's sleep I have ever had until this day.

19

We were up and at the cook's tent early. I was itchy to get shut of the Wild West and head for the train station. D met us with the latest news. It turned out that the rifle shot we heard landed the wolf man in the dust and it was the talk of the camp. I figured I would see those eyes in my dreams for years to come. I wondered how a person ended up that way. Book said that some people get used for harm through their own choices in life. We probably would never know why we were being hunted by him. I was just glad we had help. Someone up there was watchin' out for us.

We said our goodbyes and Bill Cody lent us a wagon and driver for the trip back to town. There was a big pack-up going on everywhere we looked. I didn't even want to think about how much work it took to move a whole tent city by rail. I turned to take one last look at the Wild West. I could smell the campfires, morning grass, animals, and so many other things I could not even begin to tell ya about. I could see the small herd of Buffalo coming up over the meadow and wondered if I would ever see them wild on the prairie again. D came riding up behind the wagon on her gelding with her big smile.

"Well Cisco, was I right, or was I right?"

I was just about to answer when over the hill behind her came another horse. The rider had a bandaged head under his tall hat. I recognized the eyes right away and felt my face get hot. I was just glad he was alright.

*

Guthrie and D led the way to the train station so we could get our tickets. When we got to the booth, the ticket man recognized us right away.

"Hey, you two, I got a special order from Bill Cody." He handed us our tickets with a note.

It read, "Please except my sincere appreciation and these two first class tickets, Signed, William F. Cody."

I read it out loud and D gave a whistle. Behind us came a commotion and we turned to see a steam powered contraption rolling its way down the street. On closer inspection I could tell that it looked kinda like an undertaker's wagon, only with no horse pulling it. I already met the driver.

Vincent waved his black top hat in our direction, "Greetings gentlemen! Splendid timing once again! The steam age is upon us! We can thank the genius of Sir Charles Algernon Parson and his Multi-Stage Reaction Turbine." He looked out over a group of wide-eyed, open-mouthed onlookers. "I, too, have attended lectures on the work of James Stuart. Has no one heard of Mechanisms and Applied Mechanics? No. No one?!" He threw up his hands in frustration.

He was wearing strange purple glass spectacles. Sitting on the seat next to him was a smallish woman in all black velvet. We took a walk over to get a better look. A crowd was now forming around him. A puff of steam shot out from the side of his wagon, making everyone jump.

"Gentlemen, I have found my Anabel Lee!"

He motioned with his outstretched hand toward the young woman in black. She had beautiful creamy skin and catlike blue green eyes. Her dark hair was curled and piled up with pins that looked like the wheels in Vincent's clock. She had a fitted outfit that was pinned together at the high neck with more wheels. On her lap was a birdcage with a funny metal bird inside. It moved its metal head back and forth. She held her spectacles up to her eyes. They had one long handle on the side and were made of round red glass. She smiled without showing her teeth and wiggled her fingers at us.

Edgar flew down and landed lightly on Vincent's shoulder.

"Onward Ivy!"

"Must you always rush me, you fiendish fowl?!"

"Farewell, Frisco and friends!"

He reached down and pulled a lever. Out shot another burst of steam. I suddenly though of something I wanted to ask him and knew this was my last chance.

I ran over, "How did you know my friend Book needed to see Julius Meyer!?"

He laughed. "Funny thing, that! Why, Edgar mentioned it!"

The bird ruffled its wings and cawed in Book's direction. She lifted her hand in goodbye.

Just then we could hear the train whistle and chug its way over the bridge and into town.

*

We had our bags packed on the train and were saying our goodbyes when a pregnant Indian woman hustled by us. I could tell she was having a rough go of it. Her face was flushed red with a trickle of sweat starting down her temple. She was lugging a large bag in one hand and dragging a small crying child with the other. By the look of their clothes you could tell they had taken a beating. I found myself wondering where they came from and where they were going. I watched them as they headed toward the third class car. I looked down at the tickets in my hand.

I walked up to her and said, "Ma'am, I'd like for you to have these here tickets."

She stood there staring at them. She looked at Book and back at me. "They will not let us ride in this car."

"They will when you show them this note." I took it out and handed it to her, "Compliments of Buffalo Bill and the U.S. Government."

She looked down at the tear-streaked face of her child and back at me, "Thank you."

After they left we watched them make their way toward the first class car. The conductor read the note and helped her board the train.

I turned to Book, "I figure what we don't know won't hurt us. I had my heart set on second class travel anyway."

We bought our new tickets with the man in the booth shaking his head in wonder.

"Well D, thanks for the tour of Omaha. You ever get tired of livin' outta trunks and whatnot, hop on that gelding and come on home."

"Thank ya kindly, Cisco. I'm not like you, yet. I still have some runnin' to do, maybe someday." She looked fretful all of a sudden.

I put my hand out to her, "Well, for now, you just be a good hand."

She grabbed my hand and pumped it up and down. Her grin was back in full force, "That's all any of us can do Cisco, be a good hand."

Guthrie came up from behind her. For a minute I forgot he was there.

"We'll be seeing ya, Cisco." He stepped forward and grabbed me in a hug. My face turned a nice camp fire color.

You would have thought I was in a big rush to get on that miserable train and you would be right. I'm glad my good friend and riding partner didn't mention it.

20

I wished I could say that my earlier ticket give away made the trip home easier. I'd like to tell ya that because we were headed home it was any better. It was no for two on both counts. It was like the same miserable, smelly group just waited for us to get back on and go the other direction.

Same routine; beefsteak, fried potatoes, fried eggs, no thank you on the prairie dog stew, gas lamps at night, boards to sleep on, dust, stink. We went right through a train stop in a town that had been wiped clean by a tornado. There were people and animals running every which way.

We sorta chugged by real slow, takin' it in like we were watching a stage play. I saw one old man smoking a pipe, rocking in a chair, and reading a paper on a porch. No house, just the porch was left; like someone stole the house and he didn't know it was missing.

My ribs were still sore and I could find no comfort from it. I was sure looking forward to getting back to the ranch. I figured I needed to have Leon give me the look-over. Who knew what kind of doc they had back at the Wild West. I threw up a little prayer for relief. It couldn't hurt.

*

I must have nodded off because Book was soon shaking my shoulder and pointing out the window. We were pulling into our own town station. Sitting tall on our wagon was the Colonel herself with a couple of twin girls we raised at the ranch. The Red was tied to the back of the wagon.

We were packed up to head out when the train whistle blew. I turned to see the great Union Pacific pull off down the tracks. I could see the windows of the first class car passing and the face of the Indian woman smiling in my direction. She held her hand to the window in a wave.

The ride back to the ranch was painful but I smiled with every bounce. We came down the hill to the Flying Bird Ranch. I could see the green valley, our fences and barn, the square box ranch house, and our herd grazing. There was a little wisp of smoke trailing into the sky from the chimney and the most wonderful smell of something cooking. Book and I looked at each other.

The Colonel blew out a puff of her cigar and smiled, "Our new gal has been giving Chop a run for his money in the culinary arts. Tonight we are having fried chicken and Chinese noodles."

I rode up closer, "You mean that gal you were cleaning up when we left?"

The twins nodded their heads up and down at the same time.

The Colonel said, "You two will just have to see for yourselves."

*

Once word got around we were ridin' in, we had a little welcome crowd gathered on the front porch. There were hands grabbing our bags for us and questions flying from everywhere at once.

There was so much ruckus that the Colonel held up her hands and finally yelled, "Just one minute here! Let's let these gals get settled first! We can all have a good story at supper."

The front door banged open and out stepped Leon, who came over smiling. I pulled the package and note from my bag that Lung Hay gave me and handed it over to him.

I said, "Doc Hay says you need to practice your Chinese by reading this note to me."

He chuckled and gave me a hug. I pulled back a little because of the pain in my ribs. He noticed and looked at me fretfully.

I patted my ribs and told him, "Just some bruises."

He raised his eyebrows at me, "We will see."

There was another bang of the door and a black woman stepped out wiping her hands on her apron. Her hair was neatly pulled up and she had a little more pink color to her cheeks. Gone was the pasty look that she had when I first saw her. She looked a little tired, but much younger than before. She held out her hand gently to me, like she might break or something if I squeezed too hard.

"You must be Cisco. My name is Tatum, Tatum Love. I want to thank you all for having me. Lord knows I was a trouble. I come a long way to come to this here place." She had a sweet smile.

I reached for her hand, "Tatum Love, we all came a long way to get to this here place, welcome."

21

Fried chicken and Chinese noodles were now my favorite meal and made even better by the addition of Chinese sweet tea. It seemed that our two cooks were busy swapping recipes while we were away. We payed our dues and told the tales of our adventures to a wide-eyed audience. Everyone had to try out Books new spectacles and run their fingers on the white feather in her hat, a gift from Looking Glass. They made me tell the story of Kiddo the monkey over and over again. When I did, they'd look over at Book who would nod her head in agreement just to back my story. Keyes made a big fuss over the cutters that Veloria gave us and made a solemn vow to keep up the trims as needed.

There was no smoke for me on the porch that night. We both got long, hot baths in the Flying Bird claw foot tub. You didn't think we were fool enough to get rid of that did you? I got poked and checked over and sent to my bed in the room I shared with my good friend and riding partner. I was smiling all the way till I fell asleep that night.

*

I must have slept the whole next day. At night I found my way to Leon's room. His walls were covered with book shelves that smelled of tobacco, tea, and incense. He was sitting in his high-backed chair reading under an oil lamp. I came up behind him and he took a puff at his long pipe.

He read, "Dear Lee On, I was concerned for your safety when I received news that a number of Chinese had been killed in the mining camps. It grieves me to say that it is not safe for any of us in these times. I was happy to hear of your success and good health. You have friends that love you and that is all we can ask for in this life. I hope our paths will again cross some day. You have your work and I have mine. Please enjoy these books. They have given me great pleasure. Remember my friend; one thousand years ago we were all one family. You're Friend, Lung Hay."

When he was done reading, he took another puff at his pipe.

I said, "Do you know that your friend packs a six gun?"

He smiled and took another puff of his pipe.

Afterwords...

Time passed and we got back into our routine of work on the ranch. My ribs had long since healed, thanks to the care of Leon. The Colonel and I were having our evening smoke on the porch. It was an Indian summer and the sky looked afire with reds, pinks, and oranges. A star twinkled, then another. We heard the door bump open and out came Tatum, our newest edition.

"Pull up a chair, Tate. Would you like a smoke?"

"Nooo. Thank you kindly, Colonel." She nodded to me and I nodded back. "It's such a blessed quiet here, not like in the city."

"What's it like there, Tate?" I asked. Then I remembered the Colonel saying she came from San Francisco too, like Leon, and so many others.

"They say that yonder city is the haunt of the low and the vile of every kind; thief, house burglar, tramp, whore, cutthroats, murderers, dance halls, concert saloons, gambling houses full up with riot-loving rowdies in all states of intoxication, opium dens, disease, insanity, pollution, and Hell is there too."

All the time the Colonel was nodding her head in agreement. That was enough for me.

She went on, "They hung my momma in the South, for what I don't know. Next I knew my brother and I got separated. I was sent through the Underground Railroad to work for Mam Pleasant. She educated me to work for rich white folks. Sometimes the men would take advantage of me. Laudanum did not help me to forget enough and keep on. I got some money saved and left."

"How did you know to come here?" I asked her.

"Well now, you all didn't think your Flying Bird was a secret? The good Lord has His ways of workin,' and don't you think He don't." She winked at me.

"Did you ever find your brother?"

"Oh yes, child. He came out West. Ain't you ever heard of the famous cowboy Nat Love?"

After she left I thought about what she said, even when I was back in my room that night. The crickets sang from outside. The late summer moon strolled across the sky. It was then I thought about Guthrie.

I said to Book across the room, "I wonder why they call him Jigsaw?"

She said, "D told me that it was because they had to keep putting him back together after his rides. You can ask him yourself soon. She told me she was going to bring him for a tour of the ranch the next time she comes back."

I was glad it was dark because my face was burnin' up.

Another book by S. Southcott

On the Trail with Cisco Peach
I SBN: 978-0-6152-1632-4
A Star Brand® Dime Novel
Check it out @
www.freewebs/ssouthcott.com
www.myspace.com/2gunshu
Amazon.com

www.ingramcontent.com/pod-product-compliance
Lightning Source LLC
Chambersburg PA
CBHW030146200626
46812CB00015B/1713